HONEY GLAZED

THE CONTINENTAL BREAKFAST CLUB - BOOK THREE

PAMELA FORD

AINE PRESS

No part of this book may be used or reproduced in any manner whatsoever without written permission except in the case of brief quotations embodied in critical articles and reviews.

This is a work of fiction. Names, characters, places, and incidents are either the products of the author's imagination or are used fictitiously. Any resemblance to actual events, locales, organizations or persons, living or dead, is entirely coincidental.

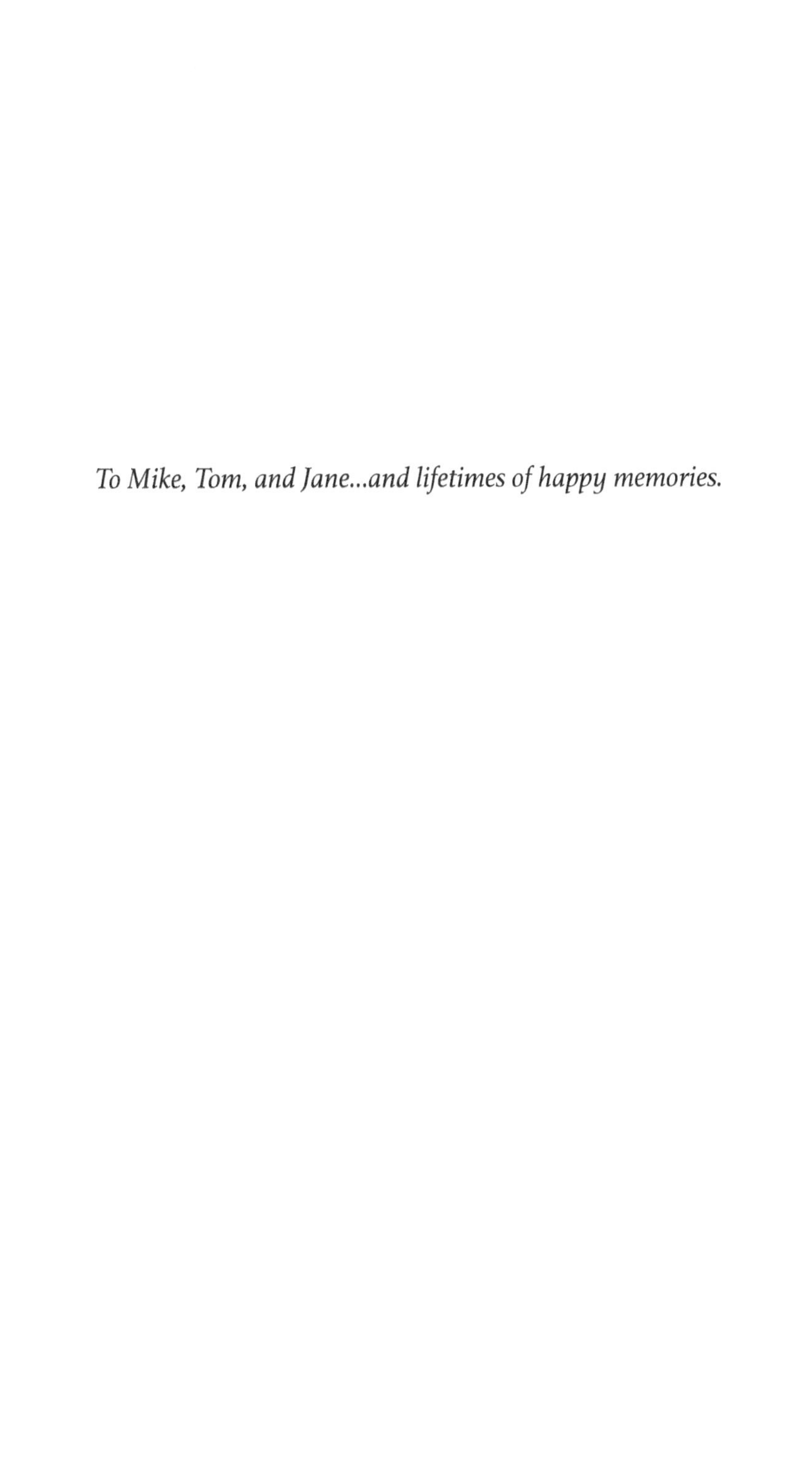

To Mike, Tom, and Jane...and lifetimes of happy memories.

ONE

"I'VE SEEN YOU AT CONTINENTAL BREAKFAST THREE TIMES this week," he said. "At three different hotels..."

There was no reason to panic. Maybe I'd misunderstood the question. Maybe he'd said something other than what I thought I'd heard. "Excuse me?" I said with forced pleasantness to the handsome guy wearing khakis and a white shirt who had slid—without invitation—into the chair across from me at breakfast.

"You've been at breakfast at three different hotels this week."

My heart dropped. That's what I thought he said. I tried to quiet the alarms going off in my head. Why had this guy been at all the same continental breakfasts as me? How had I not noticed him? No, really. *How had I not noticed him?* He was ruggedly handsome—dark brown hair, brown eyes framed by cool glasses, dark stubble on a strong jaw, in decent shape, and definitely in my target age range. At the very least, he would have been worth a second look. Honestly, this guy hit all the marks so well he might even have warranted a Continental Breakfast Club question of the day: *Do you mind if I share your table?*

Not that any of that mattered at this point. What really mattered was: who was he, what did he want, and why, oh why, hadn't I given more credence to Megan, Allie, and Bree's warnings?

"Most important meal of the day," I said with a spindly laugh.

I could almost hear Megan adamantly saying, "Kristin, when you're sneaking into continental breakfast at nice hotels, stay alert. You don't want the staff figuring out you slipped in the side door when someone else exited."

To which Allie had added, "The last thing you need is the manager discovering you're not even staying at the hotel—that you're there trying to meet single men."

After which Bree had put the cherry on the sundae: "Whatever you do, don't let security discover you're hanging with the paying guests and eating for free. Because to them it'll be theft, plain and simple."

"I have a purpose for being here..." I began slowly. My thoughts started to sprint the interior perimeter of my skull, picking up speed with each passing micro-second. Oh God, could Bree have been right? Could this guy be security? In khakis and a white shirt?

Yes, of course, my mind screamed. Security at upscale hotels wouldn't be decked out in blue, police-style uniforms with big, black leather holsters. That would be too conspicuous. At places like this, security probably dressed to blend in to maintain the illusion of privilege and privacy. But if he was on security detail here, then why had he been at all the other hotels? My brain skidded to an abrupt halt as the answer exploded like a single firework in my frontal lobe.

Outsourcing.

Of course. It made perfect sense. The hotels were outsourcing their security. Everything was outsourced these days. Why not security? It was probably the ideal way for hotel management to ensure they had perfectly-trained, razor-sharp response teams.

I eyed the man across from me again. My stomach fluttered. He did look razor-sharp, I granted him that. Maybe he was a supervisor from the security firm. Maybe even the owner. Either of those totally explained why he'd been at three different hotels this week. He'd probably been making the rounds to do things like...assessing his employees and ensuring security at each hotel remained, well, secure.

"A purpose?" he pressed, no doubt expecting to hear a rational explanation for why I'd apparently stayed at a different hotel every night this week and, thus, was at a different continental breakfast every morning. As I frantically searched for any remotely believable reason to give him, I counted myself lucky that he'd only seen me at three breakfasts because, in reality, I'd been at four.

Yes, I know it might sound a bit obsessive, but when I joined the Continental Breakfast Club, I decided to go in big. Figured that increasing the number of breakfasts I visited each week would exponentially increase my odds of meeting a man who actually had his act together.

I was just so sick of dating guys who needed saving. My brothers say it's my own fault, that I have the *save the world* gene. And they may be right about that. But I'm happy to report that I'm truly ready to find a stable guy and leave *saving the world* to someone else.

After the silence had gone on too long, and I accepted the fact that a good excuse wasn't going to magically insert itself into my head, I raised my chin and went on the offensive. "And you are?" I asked, inserting a hint of offended snootiness into my voice.

"Oh, sorry. I'm Drew." He smiled and reached across the table to shake my hand.

His manner was open, his brown eyes friendly and unthreatening. He seemed like just a regular guy, albeit very, um...attractive and masculine. I could see how easily he could use his charm and looks to suck people into liking him. A perfect skill for a security expert.

But he wasn't fooling me. Anyone could affect a demeanor that made them seem nice—didn't mean they actually were. As head of security, he probably trained his employees on how to disarm people's mistrust: *act approachable and put on a big, sincere smile.*

"Nice to meet you." I purposely avoided introducing myself, figuring the less he knew about me, the better. Tearing off a piece of the chocolate frosted donut on my plate, I popped it in my mouth so I had an obvious reason for not saying more.

"Good donuts?" he asked, obviously trying to put me at ease so I'd give up the information he wanted.

I was *so* onto him.

Wait. Did he say donuts, *plural?* As in, more than one? Was he asking a general question—or did he know this was my second donut today? My face flushed. *Did he know I'd had two at every continental breakfast this week?* Okay fine, yesterday I had three, but the third one hardly counted because I took it with me to have later.

Did continental breakfast have limits? Fair share rules? Donut allotments? Did the rich do continental breakfast differently than the rest of us?

I nodded and swallowed the bite of donut. "Delicious. Best donuts in the world," I said, as though it totally explained my gluttony just in case he was aware of it. I almost added, *I can't stop eating them,* but realized in the nick of time that it made me sound a bit unhinged even though it was the truth.

Let me clarify. These donuts weren't those boxed, store-bought numbers you get at cheap motel breakfasts. You know, the kind with frosting that looks and feels like sprayed-on wax, especially the chocolate ones. No, these were obviously made fresh every morning. Sometimes they were still a little warm. Each one was light and pillowy, covered in buttercream frosting or sweet sugar glaze that made it impossible not to lick your fingers afterward in a desperate quest for just one more taste.

"So, I have to admit..." Drew said. "I've been trying to figure out what you're up to. I came up with a couple of theories... But when I spotted you going in the side door this morning, well, that clinched it."

My heart thudded against my ribcage. My hands started to sweat. He knew? *He knew I was sneaking in?* Shit, next he would want to know why I was doing it—and no way was I telling the truth. It would be too humiliating, not to mention, potentially illegal. I had to come up with a really good excuse, one that would make him shake his head in sympathy, pat me on the arm, and send me along with a simple warning not to do it again.

"I'm just having breakfast," I said in a thin voice, trying to appear unfazed as I debated what response would garner the most empathy.

"At a different hotel every day?" His gaze sharpened on mine.

Should I say I'd lost my job and didn't have any money to buy food? Or that I was a college student and used every penny to make rent? Or, or—how about that I'd committed too much of this week's paycheck to charity and had nothing left for myself.

Okay, so that last one might be going a bit far.

My heart felt like it was about to crash through my chest wall, and for some reason, my mouth was refusing to work. I closed my eyes a brief second to regain control. *Theft. You're stealing from these hotels.* What was the penalty for stealing? A monetary fine? Jail? Was taking breakfast considered grand theft? It didn't seem to be on the same scale as stealing cars and boats and million dollar jewelry.

Although these donuts, I had to admit, were pretty damn *grand*.

Drew sat back in his chair and crossed his arms over his chest. "I know exactly what you're up to."

I stared back at him, feeling like a guillotine was about to land on my neck. How could anyone so handsome be an executioner?

"It's because of my job," I began, intending to explain how I was out of work and out of food. Once I made my case, I would get up and leave before he had time to check out my story.

A slight smile turned up the corners of his mouth, and he held up one hand to stop me. "I know what you're doing," he said in a low voice. "You're writing a review. You're a reviewer."

It took a moment for my brain to register his words. A reviewer? He thought I was a reviewer? *A reviewer!* Giddy joy surged through me and I suppressed the urge to laugh. He thought I was reviewing the hotel—maybe even the breakfast. And yes! I was! Of course I was! I wrote reviews! I was a reviewer! *A reviewer!*

"Guilty," I said, beaming at him.

"Ha! Thought so. Couldn't figure out any other reason why you'd be at so many different hotels in one week." He grinned back at me. "Well, I could think of one...but you didn't look like that kind of girl."

A guffaw burst out of me, too loud, and I quickly pulled it back in. He had no idea how close to the truth he'd come; after all, I *was* looking to meet men, just not for that reason. "No, no, not me! I'm here strictly for—" I glanced to either side and dropped my voice. "—reviewing reasons. I'm supposed to be incognito. So could you please...what I mean, is...we would really appreciate...if you could keep this information confidential."

"We?"

"Oh I mean, me." I bobbed my head up and down. "And the review site. I'm doing a comparison story about the best hotel continental breakfasts in the area." Shit, oh shit, oh shit. What was the name of that website everyone seemed to be talking about these days? The one that offered an app to help plan your trip? I clenched my teeth.

"I do reviews for...you've probably heard of it. It's called —" I stopped, waiting for the site name to jump into the blank space in my sentence. What the hell? Normally, I'd be able to retrieve the name without giving it a second thought. But, apparently, my mental recall was under so much duress at that moment, it didn't work anymore. After another silent beat, I knew I had no choice but to leap to Plan B. "It's, ahh, an online review site called..." All I could think about was how much I wanted to get out of there and never come back. "...*Get out of Here*," I said, forcing a smile.

Get out of Here? Seriously? That was the best fake website name I could come up with?

Drew's brows pulled together, doubt flashed through his eyes. "Never heard of it."

Heat stole up my chest, and a nervous giggle trilled out of my mouth. Whoever this guy was, whatever his role at the hotel, I really needed him to buy into my story until I had a chance to escape.

"Did I say *Get out of Here?*" I burbled. My words started coming faster. "Heh, heh. My mind is totally disconnected this morning. I've had to be at the hotels right when continental breakfast opens, so I'm getting up at five every day. And I'm a night owl so I'm getting four or five hours of sleep at the most. And you know what they say sleep deprivation does to you." *Oh my God, shut up.*

I calmed my voice. "Anyway my point is, I review for —*Get out of Town*—not *Get out of Here.*"

"*Get out of Town?*" He still seemed unconvinced.

I took a deep breath and dove into the lie, nodding my head to fortify my words. "You know how people exclaim *Get out of Town!* when they're in disbelief about something? Well, my goal is to spotlight places that are so good, once people read my reviews, their first response will be, '*Get out of town!*' Which they'll quickly follow with, *I've got to give that place a try.*"

I licked my lips nervously, tasting the frosting from my donut again. No! Don't tell me I'd been blabbering away with food on my lower lip. No wonder Drew was looking at me with such a strange expression; he probably couldn't rip his eyes off the smear of chocolate, wondering how long it would take me to realize it was there. I dabbed at my mouth with a napkin.

He was just staring at me, so I jumped back in to fill the silence. "Sometimes I joke around, calling the site *Get out of Here*, so you can see how that just slipped out. I have to be careful about that. *Get out of Here. Get out of Town.* Get it?" Enough already. I glanced upward and prayed for a lightning bolt to shatter the ceiling and shut me up.

Drew leaned toward me conspiratorially, his eyes locking with mine. A shiver of attraction tiptoed up my spine. "Okay, I won't tell anyone you're doing a review...if you tell me which breakfast is best. I promise to keep your secret even under threat of death," he teased.

A bit flustered, I sat back in my chair to put some distance between us, and wagged a finger back and forth. "No, no, no. That's breaking all the rules. Anyway, it's too soon to tell. Since I need to go to each location twice, I still have plenty of research to do."

Drew nodded thoughtfully. I had the sudden suspicion that some theory was running through his head—and I didn't want to hang around to find out what it was. Time for me to get out of town before he asked any more questions.

I made a show of checking at my watch as though I had to be somewhere, even though at seven in the morning, the only place I had to be was *early for work*. Which would be okay, since I'd been late twice this week already because of continental breakfast. Not that being a little late was a big deal at *The Joneses*, the catalog where I was a merchandising assistant in the product development department. But my boss tended to make backhanded comments, and since all I wanted from the place was a better job—a scenario that had been dangled in front of me when I was hired four years ago and had not yet come to pass—it was in my own best interests to keep Carly happy.

The Joneses, in case you haven't heard of it, is the catalog you find on end tables in the airlines' elite lounges, in seat pockets in the first-class sections of planes, and in the mailboxes of the top ten percent. Hence the name, The Joneses. As in, *Keeping up with The Joneses*.

We offer unusual products that appeal to people with oodles of disposable income. Like hundred-thousand-dollar jet packs (get an adrenalin rush as you fly higher), solid gold back scratchers (get rid of that itch the King Midas way), and electronic doggie doors that are activated by the dog's collar (get your dog to let himself out). As our company CEO puts it: *We offer unconventional, high quality merchandise with intrinsic value that conveys success and sophistication.*

I've never been exactly sure what that bit about intrinsic value means, but since it sounds impressive, I always mention it when I'm asked about the company. Sometimes when I'm feeling down that I can't get promoted, I say it out loud because it makes me feel like I'm part of the catalog's *in* group—the management team and their favored employees.

Say it out loud once and you'll see what I mean. *Intrinsic Value.* Feel the power?

I pushed back my chair, picked up my briefcase and put the strap over my shoulder. "It's been really nice talking to you, Drew, but I have to get to the next breakfast before all the food gets eaten." I beamed as though he and I were new friends and this conversation was the truth, the whole truth and nothing but the truth. In reality, I was shaking inside. "I'd really appreciate if you could keep my story quiet. If even a few hotels got wind of this article and changed their breakfasts for a couple of weeks, it could unfairly skew the results."

After a quick handshake, I strode out of the breakfast room and across the lobby, mentally counting my steps...*fourteen, fifteen, sixteen, seventeen*...to keep my nerves contained until I got to my car. Wait until Megan, Allie, and Bree heard about my close call with hotel security, they were going to—

"Are you really going to leave behind one of the best donuts in the world?"

Whaaat? My stomach flopped as Drew fell in beside me. He held out my donut wrapped in a white paper napkin.

My cheeks began to color. "I, um, didn't know if I could take food out or not."

"Of course you can," he said as we pushed through the double doors side-by-side.

"I don't think they'd like you taking out a tray of food, but a donut?" He shook his head. "Anyway, since here we are again... I have this idea. Something I want to ask you."

My heart rate accelerated. What? I couldn't handle any more questions about what I was doing here. I looked at him sidelong, and my romantic side leapt forward. What if he wanted to ask me out? What if this man with deep brown eyes that sparkled with flecks of gold, and a smile that promised untold pleasures just wanted a date with me? Was that too unbelievable to consider?

Waait. Waaaaaait. He was a security guard. I was lying about being a reviewer. And since those two factors were irrefutable, anything other than *goodbye* from this admittedly handsome man couldn't be good. *No ideas allowed. No questions,* I wanted to say. But I kept my mouth shut and quickened my pace. Didn't he have more important security things to do at the hotel than chase—and possibly arrest—a breakfast interloper? At that thought, I stepped into high gear. If I didn't get out of here soon, I was going to have to tell the girls that the only date I'd gotten through the Continental Breakfast Club was a court date with the District Attorney.

"Here's the thing," he said, matching me stride-for-stride. "I'm happy to keep your review story a secret. No worries about that. And, I honestly don't expect anything in return. But these days, reviews are really important. And we could sure use one."

"And you're getting one." The lie skated out of me so naturally, I actually believed it myself for a moment.

"Not the hotel." He gestured toward a white panel truck parked ahead, the side of which was painted with a huge, pink frosted, sprinkle-covered donut missing a bite. The words, *Grandad's Donuts*, were emblazoned above it in green.

I stopped and glanced from the truck to him and back again, confusion blurring my thoughts. Was this a surveillance van? Did his security company disguise its vans as donut trucks? "Is that a—"

"Delivery truck."

"Right. But is it really a sur—"

His expression told me everything I needed to know. I was a moron. This guy wasn't in security. He was a bakery deliveryman.

A damn good looking bakery deliveryman, I might add.

Clearly, lack of sleep was slowing the cogs in my head like they were covered in molasses. "You're the donut delivery guy," I said, gesturing toward the truck with the donut he'd handed me. Suddenly everything was making sense—him being in all the hotels, asking whether I liked the donuts…

He nodded. "Opened six months ago. But the owner's had a tough time getting the word out."

"How can that be? His donuts are in so many continental breakfasts." I turned toward the hotel front entrance. "Think of all the travelers getting introduced to the delectable taste of Grandad's Donuts every morning."

"Yeah. Except the key word is *travelers.* Hotel guests don't live in town. Supplying continental breakfasts brings in revenue, but it doesn't deliver repeat sales because the people eating the donuts don't live here."

I nodded empathetically, anxious to make my break. "I'm sure it's just a matter of—"

"Anyway, when I realized you were a reviewer…" He raked his fingers through his hair. "I thought, maybe you could help."

This couldn't be happening. "You want me to review Grandad's Donuts?"

"Could you?"

There was so much hope in his brown eyes, the word *yes* was tumbling through my bloodstream like it was a fat globule from all the donuts I'd eaten. But even though I wished there were some way I could agree to do it, self-destruction wasn't on the agenda today. I mean, how could I promise a review on *Get out of Town* when the website didn't even exist? "I don't think that would be poss—"

"Grandad's Donuts are in at least a few of the hotels you're reviewing," he interrupted. "You called them *delicious*. Said they were, *the best donuts in the world*. Using that measure, it seems possible that hotels offering Grandad's Donuts might be ranked higher in your article. And if that ends up the case, wouldn't it make sense that Grandad's deserves a mention in your story? Maybe even a sidebar."

I blinked. Twice. What was I supposed to say? This guy was a hell of a salesman. And, he was right. A sidebar about these amazing donuts would be the perfect accompaniment to a story about hotel continental breakfasts. *If such a story was really in the works.*

I opened my mouth to shut the idea down, but before I could get out a word, he held up a hand.

"Wait. Don't say no yet. Why don't you follow me to the bakery and talk to the owner, Nate? Find out what makes these donuts different."

Sweat popped out across my shoulders and prickled under my arms. I was touched that he wanted to help his employer...but, obviously, I wasn't in a position to help. I opened my hands, palm up, the napkin-wrapped donut clutched between the thumb and index finger of my right hand. "If I had time, maybe, but I have to get to another hotel."

"I can appreciate that," he said, and I totally knew he didn't. For a donut delivery driver he sure knew how to go after what he wanted. "But there's a reason these high-end hotels feature Grandad's Donuts. Put any donut up against Grandad's and it'll lose. Nate is a great guy, he's working hard to make this business go. Giving him some good publicity would be kind of like doing a community service."

I squeezed the donut in frustration, compressing the fluffy dough almost flat. All I'd wanted to do was meet a guy who had his act together, and instead what I got was a tenacious donut delivery man. Pressing my lips together, I gathered my thoughts, prepared to say whatever was necessary to shut this guy down. Then I leveled a firm gaze on him. "Look," was all I got out before his expression stopped me.

His face was so full of optimism and enthusiasm and determination and, oh shit, suddenly he looked so cute that even though I knew I couldn't deliver a review because I didn't really work at a review website, and even though I knew that I had vowed to quit trying to save the world, somehow when I was about to say I didn't have enough time to stop by the bakery, what came out was, "I guess I could swing in there for a few minutes."

I figured all I had to do was take a peek around, ask a few questions, promise to consider adding information about Grandad's Donuts to my continental breakfast review story, and then get out. That would be that. No mess, no fuss, no problem, no one the wiser—and everyone just a little happier.

For a while anyway.

There was the small matter of Nate and Drew expecting to actually see a review, but I decided to ignore that train of thought.

"Follow me," Drew said as he climbed into the donut truck.

I had barely pulled out behind him when reality burst through my wall of denial. Drew didn't know my name—and I was safe as long as he didn't. But if I went to the bakery, at some point I'd have to introduce myself. Everyone would know I was Kristin Caruso. Suddenly I'd be trackable. One Google search later, they would begin to figure out that I didn't work as a reviewer. Two Google searches later, they would discover there was no *Get out of Town* website.

That would be the moment someone would ask me to clarify the web address. I clutched the steering wheel more tightly. More lies would be necessary. I'd have to act surprised that the site was down and wonder aloud if it had been hacked. Or say it was undergoing maintenance. Or maybe that it was being redesigned. Or—a novel idea struck me—I could admit I'd made everything up, that I wasn't a reviewer, that I didn't work at a review site, and the real reason I was at a bunch of continental breakfasts was because I was desperately trying to meet single men.

My blood froze with mortification. Tell this handsome

stranger the real reason I was at continental breakfast? No way. I couldn't admit the truth—and, frankly, there was no reason he had to know it. Sneaking into continental breakfast at posh hotels so you can meet single men just wasn't the kind of thing any woman should ever admit to —especially not to a guy who looked like Drew.

Panic reared its head. Nothing I'd been discussing with Drew was real. Nothing. How had I let myself get into this mess? How had I let his charming smile convince my *save the world* predisposition that it was a good idea for me to go to the bakery?

I didn't even need to call Allie, Megan, and Bree to know what they would say: get out of this right now.

Get out. I gulped in a breath, then eased up on the gas pedal to let a few car lengths open between my car and the donut truck. A green minivan slid into the space in front of me, and I dropped further back, biding my time. When the donut truck traveled through the next green light, I knew the right moment had arrived. I followed the truck into the intersection, then spun my steering wheel into a sharp right turn, put my foot to the pedal, and disappeared into the city.

Thank God, I had come to my senses just in time.

TWO

TWO WEEKS LATER, I HAD MANAGED TO SEAL MY DISTRESSING Grandad's Donuts incident into a mental lockbox and bury it in a deep corner of my mind. The only time *The Incident*, which is what I had taken to calling it, ever made its way into my consciousness was when one of the girls tried to convince me to give continental breakfast another chance.

I'd met the three of them on Hatteras Island last month when I was vacationing with my family at my grandma's beach house. We bonded like we'd grown up together, and when they told me about the Continental Breakfast Club, well, of course I wanted in. I hadn't told any of my other friends about continental breakfast thinking I'd wait to see how well it worked. Obviously, it had been a bit traumatic, so even more obviously, I was keeping the experience confined to Megan, Allie, Bree, and me.

Anyway, that's where I found myself, once again, after taking a call from Bree early on a Friday morning.

"Once bitten, twice shy," I said as I brushed on mascara, frowning as some of my eyelashes stuck together in clumps. Obviously, it was time for new mascara. "Don't you have math classes to teach?"

"Teacher in-service. High school's closed today," Bree said. "Now, Kristin listen. I get why you're afraid to try again, but I have an absolutely brilliant idea that will remove all your post-traumatic Grandad's Donuts stress."

"I don't have post-traumatic stress." I dug out my eyelash comb and used it to separate the clumped lashes. "I have Drewaphobia. As in, I never want to run into that Drew guy again."

"My idea will help either way," Bree said. "How about if I call all the hotels on our list to find out which ones feature Grandad's Donuts? Then you only go to continental breakfast at the ones that don't. If Grandad's aren't on the buffet, you can't possibly run into Drew. What do you think?"

"That's a thought," I said, running a brush through my wavy, shoulder-length hair. Dark brown hair, dark brown eyes. Kind of boring. Sometimes I wished I could be a blue-eyed blond, but my Italian heritage pretty much put the kibosh on that.

"Think how well it worked out for me. Because of continental breakfast, I'm dating Adam. And look at Allie —she met Jax. So you want to try again?"

"Not really." What I wanted to do was forget all the lies I'd said that morning. "I'm lucky I escaped with my life the last time."

Bree snorted. "Nice exaggeration. Come on, you just said, *That's a thought.*"

"*That's a thought* is a nice way of saying *no.*"

When Bree didn't answer, a twinge of guilt poked at me. I knew she was only trying to help, that she just wanted me to find an awesome guy like she had.

I exhaled dramatically. "Fine, I'll think about it," I finally said, figuring that would be good enough to put her off for a while. "I have to go. I can't be late today. This morning is the annual employee meeting where they tell us how well the company did last year and hand out bonuses and stuff."

"I thought you said sales were down."

"Yeah, I know." I pursed my mouth in dismay. "But they say that every year, and then at bonus time everything is roses. I think emphasizing the negative is just one of the CEO's weird attempts at motivation. Don't forget, this is the same guy who brought in actors dressed like cops to deliver our bonuses one year. We thought the company was under investigation and we were being subpoenaed. He thought it was hilarious."

I shrugged into a bright, salmon-colored jacket with three-quarter-length sleeves and rolled the cuffs of my white blouse over the top of the jacket sleeves. Twisting to one side and then the other, I checked my outfit in the mirror. Stylish gray skirt, white top, salmon jacket. Not too dressy, not too casual. A great professional ensemble for the company meeting. Maybe this year someone would actually take notice and think to themselves, *We should promote that girl.*

Since *The Joneses* wasn't a huge company—about a hundred and twenty five employees strong—we all gathered in the warehouse for the annual meeting, coffee cups in hand. The atmosphere was jovial; after all, if this year followed the same pattern as past years, we were about to learn that each of us would be getting a check for at least several thousand dollars.

The company CEO stepped onto the stage that had been set up for the presentation; his silver hair glinted under the bright lights. Everyone applauded as he walked slowly to the podium, and I exchanged a cheeky grin with my co-workers, Melanie and James. All week we'd been discussing what we'd do with this year's bounty. Melanie was planning a trip to Sweden to trace her ancestry, and James wanted to buy season football tickets. For me, it would be nothing too exciting. My car needed brakes and my credit card needing paying down, so I hoped to use my bonus to get back to square one.

James opened a bakery bag, pulled out a muffin the size of a softball and held it toward me to see if I wanted a bite. The guy was always eating something fattening but he stayed skinny as a rail. Maybe it had something to do with being about six foot three. Totally unfair, since I was barely five foot four and was always fighting five pounds.

I shook my head. "I had toast this morning."

Anyway, once I got myself on stable ground with the bonus, I was determined to turn over a new financial leaf. No matter how hard it got, I was going to control my spending and live within my means. Which, admittedly, might be somewhat tough, because even though The Joneses sold expensive products targeted toward the extremely well-to-do, the catalog didn't pay merchandising assistants all that well.

"Another 365 behind us." The CEO's voice rocketed out of the PA system, repeating the same phrase he started his speech with every year. "It's a big anniversary—year thirty for The Joneses. We're all a little older, a little wiser, hopefully richer in love, and not poorer in the pocketbook."

I held myself back from rolling my eyes. Yep. Same speech every year. I took a sip of my coffee and let my thoughts drift as he began to run through the year-end review. The program always followed the same format. After finishing the review, he would thank us for another fantastic year, then call a few people up on stage to receive achievement awards that were appropriately named *Going Above & Beyond the Joneses*.

Melanie, James, and I had long ago given up on getting

an award. Only managers or higher ever got recognized. No big deal; if I had to choose, I'd rather get a promotion than an award any day.

Although, obviously, I hadn't gotten a promotion either. But on the silver lining side, not ever getting recognized meant I never had to worry about whether I had a thank-you speech prepared or had dressed well enough to go on stage.

I probably sound like I don't like working at The Joneses, but honestly, I do. Really. It's just that the place has a sort of old-school caste system and I'm on the bottom tier—a member of *the unrecognizables*—which sometimes makes me feel like the job I want might never come my way. Not to mention earning a reasonable salary.

Melanie leaned toward me. "Think C.B. will get an award this year?" she asked, using the nickname James had given our boss after she'd stolen one of his ideas and passed it off as her own. C.B. stood for *Carly the Bitch*.

"When hasn't she gotten one? They love her," I said in disgust.

Carly was one of those people who had been handed many of life's benefits—beauty (of the straight black hair and blue eyes variety), brains, and a good body—and she used them to effectively stomp over everyone below her as she climbed the ladder to success. Now in her late thirties, she was not-so-subtly angling for a vice president position. The three of us had no doubt she would eventually get it.

Which was fine with me. Because even though she

would be higher up in the company—and, thus, able to continue showering some degree of misery upon me—at least it would open a spot that James or Melanie could move into. Which meant one of their jobs would open up for me to move into.

So, much as I hated Carly, I was rooting for her advancement.

Just as expected, Carly's name was called and she carried her willowy body up to the stage to accept a *Going Above & Beyond the Joneses Achievement Award* for dedication and innovation.

I set down my coffee cup and clapped heartily so it appeared that I thoroughly admired the woman, though nothing could be further from the truth. Carly was obviously a successful adherent of the career advice Melanie had spotted in a magazine: *make yourself unforgettable and irreplaceable.*

My feet were already starting to hurt from wearing heels—not the best choice for a morning spent standing on concrete in the warehouse. I shifted my stance to relieve the pressure on my toes. Melanie pointed at her own feet, happily tucked into ballet flats, and gave me a fake smug look. "Fashion before comfort," I whispered, even though I didn't totally believe it.

As soon as they finished giving out the recognition awards, then would come the real fun, that moment when the CEO announced the bonus percentage. In the four years I'd been working at The Joneses, bonuses had never been less than five percent of income. Of course, five percent of a gazillion dollars is a lot more than five percent of what I make, but since most companies don't even give bonuses to people at my level, I'm just happy to be included.

My first year, the bonus was fifteen percent, the last two years were five, so I was crossing my fingers and saying my prayers that we'd get ten percent this year. Once in a while, I would let myself dream big—of a return to fifteen percent—which would enable me to take care of my brakes, my credit card debt, and maybe even plan a vacation somewhere other than my grandma's beach house.

The CEO's voice broke my thoughts: "...hasn't been what we expected and, I'm sorry to announce, there will be changes."

What? *What?* Changes? What wasn't as expected? What was he talking about? I tried to catch someone's attention so they could fill me in with a quick whisper. Instead, all I saw were furrowed brows and deepening frowns, all eyes riveted on the stage. Melanie's mouth hung open in shock.

Heart thudding, I fixed my attention squarely on the stage and waited.

"All of you have been like family to me," the CEO said. "And I hope this place has felt like family to you, too."

Family? I wasn't sure family was how I would

characterize being an *unrecognizable,* but I guess it was nice of him to pretend.

"So...today I come to you not just with our annual review, but also for a family meeting." His gaze slid across all of us who had gathered in the warehouse.

A family meeting? Like an intervention? Just exactly who among us was going to have to go into treatment?

"The truth is," he said, enunciating each word, "we haven't been doing well for several years. Juggling expenses, borrowing money, robbing Peter to pay Paul. I quit taking a salary a few years ago to free up revenue. And we borrowed some more, and kept paying bonuses because, hell...we're family and family takes care of one another. I was certain each new year would pull us into the black." He shook his head. "But it hasn't happened."

It hadn't? Was the company collapsing? Closing its doors? Selling out? Merging? Laying off people? Taking in borders? *What?* I glanced around again, but everyone's attention was riveted on the man who had founded this company three decades ago. A tear slipped down the cheek of the woman who headed up the accounting department; she'd been here since the beginning so the CEO probably really did feel like family to her. But these yearly meetings were the closest I ever got to the man, so he was more like a great uncle to me...you know, the guy you only see at Christmas or Thanksgiving and the conversation is always a bit awkward.

"The world has changed these past thirty years." He

adjusted the microphone. "Faster, and in more ways than most of us could have imagined. When we started, paper was king. Newspapers, magazines, catalogs. Today, if you're not online you're not alive. The Joneses has been slow to get to that party. We knew it was going on, got ourselves a website, but always figured our main audience still was in the private airport lounges, in the first class airline seats, in the exclusive neighborhoods."

The screen behind him came to life with a picture of ten smartphones.

"But phones changed everything."

The shot on the screen switched to a picture of a businessman perusing his phone while buckled into a wide, first-class seat, cocktail on his tray table. "People no longer need a catalog in the seat pocket or airline lounge to entertain them while they wait—they have their smartphones."

No one had to tell me this speech wasn't going anywhere good. One look around and it was obvious that everyone had reached the same conclusion.

"I've been investigating other options for a while now. Meeting with potential partners for an influx of capital, seeking ways to reconnect with our target audience. But the bottom line is, I turned sixty-six this year. And while I've never been one to run from a challenge, I've come to realize that this particular challenge—connecting with customers in the digital world—is more than I want to take on."

At that moment, I didn't think anyone was breathing.

It wasn't like no one had ever said this very thing to him before. It wasn't as if people hadn't brought forward proposals for improving how The Joneses connected online with its target market. It wasn't as though we'd never considered doing anything differently. We had.

But to tell you the truth, management never seemed all that open to changing its vision for the catalog. So the company just kept doing business the way it always had. The lack of change is why we all assumed the financials must be still going strong.

It was obvious from the reactions that no one from the vice presidents on down to the mail room clerk had any idea this was coming. I thought to myself that if someone had the guts to pull out a phone and start taking pictures, they might end up with an award-winning photo series documenting reactions to a rapidly-changing corporate world.

Though none of us in the audience had any idea what was coming next, I was pretty sure we would all agree that bonuses were off the table. Queasiness roiled my stomach at the thought of my finances. I would have to charge the new brakes for my car...but my MasterCard was almost maxed out.

The CEO looked out over us, the one hundred and twenty five plus employees who had gradually shifted more closely together as though proximity would protect us somehow, coffee now cold in paper cups gripped tight. "It is with much sadness that I announce..."

That's when it hit me—what if The Joneses was going out of business? This couldn't be happening, I couldn't end up out of work—

"...that after today, I will no longer oversee the day-to-day operations of The Joneses, a catalog purveyor of *unconventional, high quality merchandise with intrinsic value that conveys success and sophistication.*"

The whole room gasped. Loud murmurs rumbled through the group. It didn't take a psychic to feel the alarm ripple through the room, to know the questions running through peoples' minds. Melanie grimaced at me and mouthed the word, "Layoffs."

I felt like crying. Two hours ago, I'd been planning to pay off my MasterCard; now I'd have to increase the limit just to survive.

The CEO raised his hands and patted the air to quiet us down. "Now before anyone panics, this doesn't mean we're closing our doors. The Joneses will continue under new leadership that will enable us to shift into the digital age in a big way."

"What about our jobs?" a man near the front called out.

"They're safe. At least for the short term. But starting next week, group interviews will be conducted with each department to determine how existing employees may fit with the new company direction and philosophy."

May fit? New philosophy? What the hell was he talking about? All he'd mentioned was expanding our online presence. Did he mean something more?

"No layoffs will occur until all interviews are completed," he said.

"But, there will be layoffs?" a burly warehouse guy shouted from the back of the room.

"Not necessarily."

Oh yeah right. I could already feel my credit card limit closing in on me like spike-embedded walls. If I didn't have a job, I wouldn't be able to raise my credit limit. I gulped in some air. Okay okay okay. No need to freak out yet. I just needed to apply for an increased limit immediately. Today. Before any news of this hit the streets—or the media.

But what if the credit card company denied me an increase? Oh, they wouldn't do that, would they? I was a good customer; I'd get an increase. Except, a bigger limit meant higher payments. I couldn't afford higher payments. I could ask my parents for help. Oh please, I didn't want to go there again. At some point, I had to be an adult who took care of her own life.

My breath started coming so short and quick, the room began to spin. James spotted my distress and thrust his crumpled bakery bag at me. I dumped out the crumbs and shoved the little bag over my nose and mouth, taking deep inhales and exhales in an effort to regain normal respiration. Meanwhile, the CEO was droning on about how grateful he was for all the wonderful years and the memories would stay with him always, blah, blah, blah.

Easy for him to say—he was retiring with a ton of money, while the rest of us were just hoping to have a paycheck in a few weeks.

"So without further ado," he said. "I'd like to introduce you to the future of The Joneses, your new president...my oldest son, Andrew Lawson. Andrew brings to the job eight years of outstanding success on Wall Street."

What did a guy with Wall Street experience know about digital marketing? I pulled the muffin bag off my face and crushed it in my fist as I watched the new president stride across the stage to shake hands with the old president. The new guy was wearing gray slacks and a fitted white dress shirt, sleeves cuffed up twice. Even from the back, it was easy to see his clothes fit him well, really well—broad muscular shoulders, slim hips, tight butt. Melanie leaned in to mutter for my ears only, "Oooh, a hottie taking over the helm."

"Let's see what his face looks like before you anoint him a hottie," I murmured.

She let out a snort. "The back is good enough for me. Anyone who walks like that has to be a hottie."

The two men exchanged a few private words, then the CEO took several steps toward the rear to position himself in the background, while the new president went to the podium. His blue tie was coolly loosened at the neck, his brown hair short, his strong jaw clean-shaven. There was something really familiar about him.

"A hottie, front and back," Melanie whispered.

I nodded distractedly and squinted to see better. "Has he been in the office before?"

"I think I would remember him."

"Good morning." Andrew's voice rolled richly out of the microphone. "I apologize for the shock most of you are probably feeling right now. Hopefully this will be the last time The Joneses delivers such a surprise." He studied the podium for a moment, and I spent the subsequent pause trying to figure out why I thought I knew the guy.

"I'm extremely happy to be part of The Joneses," he said, smiling, "and looking forward to taking the catalog to a new level. I'd like to give a brief overview of my vision for the company this morning—but before we get into that, there are three points I need to cover first." He held up his index finger. "Number one: Andrew is my father's name. I go by Drew."

Realization reverberated through me like I'd just stuck my finger in an electrical outlet. Oh. My. God. *Grandad's Donuts.* The deliveryman from Grandad's Donuts? The glasses were gone from his eyes, the stubble gone from his jaw, but—shit, it was him.

What the hell was he doing here?

My thoughts began to race. Maybe it was all part of a plan. Maybe this was another of the owner's elaborate methods for delivering our bonuses. Of course. That had to be it. This Drew guy was just a starving actor who supported himself delivering donuts.

"He's not the owner's son," I whispered to Melanie, proud of my powers of deduction.

"Shhh." Her sight was locked on the gorgeous man who was supposedly taking over the company.

"He's a fraud," I hissed.

She frowned at me and gave a sharp shake of her head. "What's wrong with you?"

"He's not who he says he is."

"Shut up, Kristin," James said. "This is an opportunity."

Drew was holding up two fingers on the stage. "The second point I want to make is about company culture. After eight years on Wall Street, I'm looking forward to less duplicity and more trust. I value integrity. You'll find I'm a man of my word—and I expect the same from you."

On the screen behind him popped up a dictionary-style definition: In-teg-ri-ty (noun) – the quality of being honest and fair. Sincerity. Truthfulness. Trustworthiness.

If this was a joke, they were taking it much farther than they took the subpoena thing.

Maybe this was all just a dream. Could it be that I was still in bed, deep in REM sleep, my brain pulling together all my recent experiences into a bizarre nightmare that made no sense whatsoever?

"And the third point is this." Drew grinned and held up three fingers. "Beginning immediately, there will be a new tradition here at The Joneses. Actually, it's an old tradition that has, unfortunately, fallen by the wayside in most offices—the donut cart. Every morning, the donut cart will make the rounds of our offices, delivering fresh Grandad's Donuts—on me—free of charge—so everyone can start the morning on a sweet foot."

I wavered on my feet for a second. Then I whipped my eyes shut like I was slamming a door and pinched my forearm hard between my thumb and forefinger, certain that when I opened my eye, I would discover it was five in the morning and this was all a product of my subconscious.

Someone near me bellowed out a whoop, and my lids flew open. A few people began clapping, then others joined in, and soon there was a full-on ovation. What the hell? The guy didn't say one word about our bonuses and, yet, everyone was going nutto over free morning donuts? This *had* to be a dream.

Right?

As Drew's confident gaze drifted over the applauding crowd, reality rammed its fist into my sluggish gray-matter. This was no dream. I shoved the crumpled bakery bag in front of my mouth and nose in an absurd attempt to hide my face, and took two sideways steps to hide behind a couple of beefy warehouse men.

Oh my God. Oh my God. Oh my God. This was real. The deliveryman from Grandad's Donuts was our new president.

I was so fucked.

THREE

An hour later, Melanie rounded the corner into my cubicle practically vibrating with excitement. She tossed her blond hair. "Guess what? Nicole in HR called!" she said in a low voice. "The donut cart is coming around already! *Full of donuts!* He had it all set up in advance. Our new president really is a man of his word."

Of course he was. Of course. If he promised to do something, he would follow through. Integrity was his middle name. Sincerity. Truthfulness. Trustworthiness. Absolutely. Positively. Super-de-duper. Rah, rah, rah.

I could only imagine what his opinion was of the reviewer he'd met at continental breakfast, the one who more-or-less promised a review of Grandad's Donuts, then blew him off. He probably didn't think she was a woman of her word. Even worse, once he discovered that she was his employee at The Joneses and had made up the entire story about working for a review website, I was virtually certain she would soon be out on the street.

"Kristin?" Melanie looked at me quizzically. "You okay?"

"Did Nicole say anything about the departmental interview schedule?" I asked, desperate for the reassurance that we wouldn't have to meet with the new president for another week or two. At that moment, I had just one goal —get a temporary reprieve from the stress of knowing I would lose my job as soon as Drew recognized me.

Melanie shrugged as if to say, *what difference does it make?* "No. They probably haven't even put it together yet. But she did tell me something else. Something you're never going to believe!"

Melanie liked to keep her finger on the pulse of what was happening in the company. Unfortunately, her finger tended to typically be stuck on the pulse of all the meaningless gossip, so her knowledge wasn't all that helpful in the long term. For example, while she often was first to know who'd had a date and who was getting married, she hadn't even caught a whisper about company financial troubles or that the CEO was pulling back and his son was taking the helm.

"Whatever. Just let me know when she leaks the interview schedule." I nervously swiveled my ergonomic desk chair from side to side, taking note of a new clunking sound emanating from underneath. Great, one more problem with my chair. It was bad enough that it tilted left, and the pneumatic lift had lost its staying power so as the day wore on I sank lower and lower. But now, I clunked whenever I rotated.

The whole thing seemed like a metaphor for my life these days.

"You're going to want to know this. Guess who's pushing the donut cart."

With Drew being my new boss, this really was the least of my worries. "Nicole? The new receptionist? Really, Melanie, who cares?"

"If you were smart, you would," she said in a voice that implied that the mere act of knowing this information was about to make her head burst. I loved Melanie, but sometimes, one could only hope. I looked at her and waited.

"Okay, fine. Be that way," she said. "I won't tell you. You'll just get caught off-guard like everyone else."

"I guess that's something I'll have to live with." I turned back to my computer knowing full well that Melanie wouldn't be able to hold it in. If she knew something, she *had* to share it.

She moved closer to my desk. "Drew Lawson is delivering the donuts," she tittered. "Our new president is driving the donut cart."

I gave an exaggerated eye roll. "Good one. Oh hello, there goes a pig flying past the window."

"I'm not kidding. He is. Really." She pretended to push

a cart, nodding and smiling left and right at nonexistent people. "He told Nicole that it's an easy way for him to do a quick meet and greet. Casual, you know?"

No, I didn't know. There was no meet and greet that I was going to have with Drew Lawson that would be *casual.* Not after what I'd said and done during and after continental breakfast. "Are you serious?"

"Uh-huh." She danced foot-to-foot. "The hottie at the helm is coming around with the donuts. Nicole said that someone new would be assigned to push the cart every day. Oh! And, here's the biggest news of all—she confirmed that Drew is single."

My stomach took a lurch, and for a second I didn't know if it was because Drew was pushing the donut cart and I would have to figure out how to avoid him—or because he was single. Seriously, could this day get any more surreal?

Clearly, it was not in my best interests to run out to the cart for a donut and put myself face-to-face with Drew— and my immediate demise. "All very interesting," I said, tapping the keys on my keyboard as though I really had to get back to work. "But the last thing I need to start every day is a donut. Besides, I'm really busy today."

"Nicole said he hopes to get to every desk."

I blanched at the thought of Drew and the donut cart rolling into my workspace doorway. "This company's in trouble," I said. "Doesn't he have something more important to do than pass out donuts?"

"Yeah, I know. I guess it's about him having an open door policy. Wants to make sure he connects with everyone today, erase the levels created by job titles or something like that." She did a full-body shimmy. "I'd sure like to connect with him today even if you don't."

"Down girl." I considered what it would mean to work at a place where the chief executive not only had an open door policy, but also wanted to collapse the company organizational hierarchy. If this were true—and it was a big if—maybe he'd learned something relevant on Wall Street after all.

Melanie grew serious. "The first thing I thought was that maybe it will mean the end of the *unrecognizables*. He told Nicole he wants to get input from all the employees before he makes any hard and fast decisions."

I couldn't believe it. This company was finally going to have a president who wanted to hear from the employees —all of them—and I was going to get fired as soon as he realized who I was? How could this be happening? If I'd never gone to continental breakfast, I might finally be seeing my career path opening up. Instead, things were worse for me than they'd ever been before.

I studied my computer screen and contemplated the possibility that maybe Drew wouldn't remember what the woman he'd met at continental breakfast looked like. We'd only been sitting across from each other for a few minutes, five at most. Even when we walked outside the hotel, we were mostly standing next to each other—not facing.

Maybe it had been so early in the morning, the memory of my face was just a blur to him.

Just like the memory of his face was a blur to me. Really. All I could actually remember were the gold flecks in his brown eyes, and his strong jaw and straight nose... oh, and the little lines that crinkled in the corners when he smiled—

I sighed. Well, I could hope he didn't remember me, couldn't I? After all, I almost didn't recognize him today. Although that was more likely because he'd been wearing glasses and had the rough shadow of a beard that morning at continental breakfast. While today, he'd been clean shaven and, apparently, wearing contacts.

"Better touch-up your makeup before he arrives," Melanie teased.

"Get real, Mel, it's not a date."

A second later, an idea began to take root. Maybe some minor adjustments to my makeup would help me hide in plain sight. I could load it on in layers like Tammy Faye, so that all Drew saw was makeup and not the woman underneath.

Great idea. Except, then I'd have to become heavy makeup girl from here on out. And the thought of wearing that much makeup—let alone the amount of time it would take to put it on every morning—was enough to kill the idea in the brainstorming stage.

But what if I went makeup free?

What if I went for the laid-back natural look?

Not to brag, but my makeup at continental breakfast that morning had been impeccable. So it stood to reason that if I took the opposite makeup approach, there was a better than average chance Drew would never realize that scrubbed-clean Kristin was the sophisticated reviewer he'd met at breakfast.

I took a rubber band from my desk drawer, grabbed my purse, and pushed back my chair. "On second thought, that's a great idea," I said.

Melanie's mouth dropped open. "I was kidding."

"Many a true word is spoken in jest," I said over my shoulder as I strode from the cubicle.

In the restroom, I pumped liquid soap into my hand and scrubbed my face to remove my foundation, under eye concealer, blush, eyeshadow, eyeliner, and mascara. Black rivulets ran from beneath my lower lashes and I rubbed at them until they'd disappeared. Only when my skin was clean and I was hunched over the sink with water dribbling off my chin, did it dawn on me that the company restrooms only had air dryers. No paper towel.

I let out a sharp exhale. *What. Ever.* Dripping over to the dryer, I twisted the nozzle upward and stuck my face in the hot air. My wavy hair billowed away from the powerful blast, celebrating, no doubt, the opportunity to release itself into untamed frizz. Even though I was pretty sure a puffy mass of hair would be the crowning glory for my new plain Jane wallflower style, I couldn't do it. I grabbed my hair in a tight fist so I wouldn't have to untangle a rat's nest later.

The irony didn't escape me that I was now trying to look as unattractive as possible for a man who, two weeks earlier, I would have wanted to look my best for.

Finger-combing my hair back, I rubber banded it into a tight ponytail, then twisted it to create an austere bun at the back of my head. Three bobby pins retrieved from the bottom of my purse were enough to hold it in place. I slipped off my beautiful jacket, closed the top two buttons on my white blouse, unrolled my sleeves, and buttoned the cuffs.

Only then did I step back to take a full appraisal in the mirror. Gray skirt, white blouse, no makeup, tight hair. *Spinster librarian* was the description that leapt to mind. The only thing that might make me look more severe was a slash of cherry red lipstick, but I didn't have any...and while I did have a red permanent marker in my desk drawer which might accomplish the same thing, even I wasn't dumb enough to sentence myself to bright red lips until it wore off.

Back at my workspace, I dropped a thick stack of folders and papers on my desk so I would appear inundated by work. Then I opened my email, hoping to give the appearance I was so busy I couldn't be bothered by anything, not even donuts.

"Kristin, oh Kristin." Melanie appeared in my doorway. "The donut cart is coming down the hall," she said in a fake, joyful, we-all-work-so-happily-together voice. Her mouth dropped open. "What did you do to your hair?" she asked, all fake joyfulness gone.

"What?" I patted my hair innocently.

She waved her index finger in a quick circle at the back of her head, like she was wrapping hair into a tight bun. It's so...circa 1890."

"I saw it in a magazine," I lied. "It's the latest. Besides, I always have my hair down and sometimes it gets so...hot. Thinking I might cut it short. Or go blond." If that's what it took to keep Drew Lawson from recognizing me, it would be a small price to pay.

She narrowed her eyes. "Are you feeling okay? You look washed out. Pale."

"Yeah, I mean, no. My throat's getting sore. I might be coming down with something. I splashed cold water on my face in the restroom and that seemed to help."

"Yeah, well, I think you splashed all your makeup off."

"Oh no, really?" I asked in faux alarm. "So I look bad?"

She grimaced. "Well, you don't look good."

"You mean I look different than I do wearing makeup?" I asked. Hope sprang forth in my soul.

"Yes. Completely. When I said to touch it up, I didn't mean take it off. Get with it, Kristin, the new boss is coming around. And he's a hottie. Why would you want to be at your worst?" She pointed at my buttoned up collar and raised her brows.

"I think I'm getting the chills," I lied.

She frowned at me. "This isn't good. There's some nasty stuff going around. You want some Echinacea to boost your immune system? I've got some in my desk."

Melanie made extra money on the side as a part-time rep for a big herbal supplement company. She was always pushing something or another.

I shook my head and pointed at the bottle of water on my desk. "No thanks. I'm hydrating."

"You should take some Echinacea to nip this in the bud. If you won't think of yourself, think of the rest of us. We don't want to catch some new virus. Have you been drinking those vitamin smoothies you bought from me?"

"I keep forgetting," I said, crossing my fingers behind my back. The truth was, I tried them, but they tasted awful.

She sighed like I was some kind of hopeless case. "At least put on some blush before..."

"Donuts. Get your donuts here," a familiar voice called out from the hall as though he were hawking peanuts at the ballpark.

My heart skidded to a stop.

"Grandad's Donuts." our new president called from even closer.

Melanie contemplated me as if she wasn't quite sure what to do next. Finally she gave a defeated shrug. "Okay, forget the blush. You don't look that bad. Not really. Come on, let's go meet the boss."

I clutched my mouse in a desperate attempt to stay at my desk. Despite all the changes I'd just made in my appearance, Drew might still recognize me. I could lose my job today. I couldn't go out there. I couldn't meet him. "I've got too much work to do," I blurted. "And I'm on a diet."

"It's just one donut. Come on. We're celebrating a new day at The Joneses."

"It's not just one day. A donut is, what? Like, two hundred calories. There are two hundred and sixty work days in a year. So a donut a day is, um—" I did some quick calculations in my head. "Oh, hell, something like fifty-two thousand extra calories a year. You know as well as I do that thirty-five hundred calories adds a pound. So you want me to celebrate gaining, ah, ah—" I did some more quick math. "Oh my God, gaining fifteen pounds over the next year instead of getting a bonus check?"

Melanie exhaled and stuck her hands on her hips. "Talk about overthinking. You don't have to have a donut every day."

"Obviously you're new to Grandad's Donuts. Just wait until you try one. You won't be able to say *no* the next time." I bent toward her and lowered my voice. "Grandad's

Donuts are two-a-days, easy. Which means thirty pounds of weight gain in the next year. Think of it—*thirty pounds.*"

Melanie was staring at me like she was watching me blow up like a balloon.

"Keep the donuts," I said emphatically. "I'd rather have the cash, thank you. Plus, like I said, I think I'm getting sick." I covered my mouth with one hand and expelled a weak, sustained cough.

"What's the matter with you? Even if you're on your deathbed, you can't stand up the new president. You want to be the first person laid off?" She grabbed my arm and pulled me out of my chair.

"Okay, wait, so tell me," I said desperately. "Do I still look pale?"

She nodded. "I'm not going to lie. You look awful. Nothing like your regular self."

I'd never heard more wonderful words.

"But since Drew doesn't know this isn't what you usually look like, it doesn't matter. Come on, let's go."

I followed Melanie to where a group of employees had gathered around the donut cart out in the hall. As the smell of those incredible donuts wafted toward me, I wanted to swoon. So much for fake diets. If I got one of those sweet babes in my hands, I was going to devour every last bite. "If you get up there first, get me a honey glazed," I whispered. "So I can seem supportive," I hastily added.

People were introducing themselves to Drew,

welcoming him to the company, telling him what they did, and thanking him for the donuts. Everyone was talking and smiling and laughing and eating—it was one big, sugary love fest. Melanie went forward, and I hung back at the outside edge of the throng, still not sure this was such a good idea for me.

She reached out to shake Drew's hand. "I'm Melanie, an assistant buyer," she said. "And this is—" She turned in my direction, and I ducked down a hallway.

Absolutely not. Today was not the day I was meeting the new president. Didn't matter how little makeup I had on, how severe my hairstyle was. I wasn't ready to get recognized and lose my job. Next week would be soon enough. And since next week he would probably be pulled into all sorts of important meetings about the catalog, maybe I wouldn't have to meet him until the week after that—which would give me some time to figure out what, if anything, I could do to prevent this from becoming a full-on nightmare.

I escaped to the restroom and locked myself in a stall in case Melanie came searching for me. After several minutes of silence and no sign of Melanie, I let myself out and scowled at myself in the mirror. Touching a hand to the bun in my hair, I asked myself, "How do you get into messes like this?"

The answer came fast and hard. The problem may have begun with my lie about being a reviewer. But the real disaster arrived when I couldn't say *no* to doing a review of Grandad's Donuts—even though I had no way of actually giving the donut shop a review. My stupid predisposition toward helping was going to bring my whole world down. I was my own worst enemy. I rested my hands on the counter and dropped my head.

No more. I couldn't do this anymore. I needed to concentrate on my own life and forget about saving the world. No more jumping in to help people. No more setting up petitions to rescue the downtrodden. No more watching videos of rescue dogs and sending donations to the organizations that saved them. No more volunteering at fundraisers. No more sponsoring a child in Africa. No more forwarding online videos about captive wild animals that have never felt grass beneath their feet. No more listening to people's problems. And, especially, no more offering advice, even if people begged for it.

I was done. Just done. I was setting boundaries. Big, wide, deep boundaries. From now on, my life was going to be about me, me, and me. No more of that stupid, *save the world* bullshit. I needed to save my job and take back my life.

I pushed through the door into the hall and headed for my cubicle, confident that the donut cart was long gone.

"Kristin!" Melanie was holding open the door to the accounting department and waving two donuts in her left hand. The mere sight of those round cakes gave my spirits a lift.

"Where'd you go?" she said as I neared.

"Oh, I was there. It was just so crowded I got stuck at the back and didn't want to be the obnoxious person elbowing their way up to get a freebie."

Melanie pushed the accounting department door fully open and leaned back through the doorway. "This is Kristin, the person I was telling you about," she said over her shoulder.

Heat flashed over me. There was only one person she could be talking to—and it was the one person I didn't want to see. Before I could even take a step back, the donut cart came through the doorway followed by none other than our new president. Naturally. I wouldn't have expected anything else.

Melanie shoved the honey glazed donut into my hand and said, "Kristin, meet Drew."

I nodded, afraid to talk in case he recognized my voice.

He stuck out his hand. "Nice to meet you."

Obviously, at some point I was going to have to speak. Either that or claim spontaneous muteness, and somehow I just didn't think that would fly. "You too. I work in merchandising," I said, lowering my voice. The words came out breathy and deep. Like a porn star.

Good thing I'd buttoned my blouse up to my neck.

Melanie's brows pulled together.

I pointed at my neck. "Think I'm catching something," I said in that throaty voice.

"I offered her Echinacea," Melanie said as if that explained something.

Drew nodded slowly. I couldn't tell if it was because he didn't know what Echinacea was, or whether he was afraid I would infect him with a rare and fatal disease, or, God forbid, he was trying to figure out if he knew me from somewhere.

"It boosts your immune system," I said in an even lower voice, anxious to keep the conversation from veering into territory that included questions like, *Don't I know you from somewhere?*

"It never works for me," he said.

"Not all Echinacea is equal. It's important to buy from reputable sources because some brands don't actually contain any Echinacea at all," Melanie said in a matter-of-fact voice. "Plus, sometimes it works better in combination with lysine, vitamin C, and garlic. So you might want to try a combination."

She'd better not try selling supplements to our new president or we were all doomed. I slanted a warning look her way, and let loose a weak cough to interrupt the conversation.

Apparently she got the message, because the next thing out of her mouth was, "Drew is taking an informal poll and I told him you probably had some ideas."

Great. Just what I needed, a prolonged conversation with the man. I turned toward him, smiling apologetically. "I have a conference call coming up—"

"It's just one question," he said. "What would you say is the greatest strength—and weakness—of The Joneses?"

It may be one question, but the answer could be extensive. No way. No freaking way. The longer I stood here talking, the greater the odds he would remember me. Continental breakfast was only two weeks ago, after all. And two weeks wasn't enough time for him to forget about the reviewer who gave him the slip.

I roughly cleared my throat and pointed at my neck to make it seem like it was painful to talk. He nodded as though he had all the time in the world. It was a look I'd seen before—at continental breakfast right after he'd asked why I'd been at so many different hotel breakfasts that week. Apparently illness wasn't getting me off the hook.

Fine. I knew how to shut down this discussion; I'd just repeat exactly what the bosses had been saying forever. "Our strength is that we have an innovative product mix that appeals to people's basic need to feel like they've succeeded. Like they've *arrived*," I said in my deep, breathy voice.

"So why do you think the company is struggling?"

Ackkkk. I had some definite thoughts about this—brilliant thoughts if you ask me—but there was no way I was going there. I scrunched up my face as if to say, *Who knows?* Even though Drew was claiming to have an open door policy, he and his policies were too new. No way was going to spell out the company's shortcomings so he could label me a complainer who needed to be purged from the payroll. *Go ask the vice presidents*, I wanted to say as I kept my mouth shut.

Besides, I reminded myself, I was done saving the world. I wasn't going out on a limb, only to find the branch chopped off and myself in freefall.

"How long have you worked here?" he asked.

"Four years."

"And after four years of declining sales, you have no opinion about why the company is in trouble?" His eyes met mine in challenge and I saw what might have been construed as a flicker of recognition. Or maybe it was attraction.

Maybe he had a thing for spinster librarian types. Hahahahaha.

Of course, I had an opinion. I was *save the world girl*, wasn't I? I had opinions about everything, and this was no different. Last year, I'd shared some of my ideas during a department meeting, but I'd never taken them any further because the philosophy around here tended toward: *the bearer of bad news gets beheaded.* New ideas could be misconstrued as criticism. And I was kind of fond of my head.

Drew raised his brows, waiting. Our eyes linked and a jolt shot through me like I'd just been body slammed. My breath caught. I opened my mouth, the temptation to help overruling my determination not to. At the last second, I pulled myself back from the brink and brought my wrist up to show him my watch. "I have to run," I said. "My conference call's about to come in."

"Don't let me hold you up. We can talk about this later." Drew started down the hall pushing the cart. "Donuts here," he called out. "Best donuts in the world."

I stared after him, frozen, as I heard my words from continental breakfast roll out of his mouth.

FOUR

THE NEXT MORNING, I LAID OUT THE WHOLE STORY TO
Megan, Bree, and Allie while I was doing my regular
Saturday morning volunteer stint walking rescue dogs for
the local animal shelter. I know, I know, I vowed to quit
saving the world. But I just couldn't desert the dogs.

When the girls first learned I did volunteer dog-
walking, they signed up too, so now we meet at the shelter,
get a couple of dogs, go for a walk, drop those dogs back at
the shelter, get a couple more and walk some more.
Exercise and a good deed all rolled into one.

Anyway, we had two dogs with us that morning, both
leading the way with such enthusiasm we'd been forced
into a vigorous power walk. Allie had the leash of a
retriever type and I had a beagle mix; Megan and Bree
were behind us, dog-free. As we strode down a paved
path through the park, our conversation flowed back and

forth, crisscrossing like airplane vapor trails in the fresh air.

"You're sure he didn't recognize you?" Megan asked.

I nodded. "Wouldn't he have said something if he did? I got nervous a couple of times, thought there might be a flicker of recognition—"

"Maybe you seemed familiar, but he couldn't figure out why," Allie said.

"That's what I'm afraid of. What if it suddenly comes to him?"

The retriever bounced back toward Allie, biting and tugging at the leash. He and the beagle began to tussle with each other, tails whirling in circles of happiness. Their joy at being out of their cages was one of the main reasons I just couldn't give this up.

"No! Not now. Walk time first," Allie said with authority.

The dogs quit screwing around and ran out in front of us again.

"You're a dog whisperer," I said.

"Helps to be a groomer." She grinned. "If I don't act the alpha male, I'd never get my work done."

"Okay, enough chit-chat." Bree chopped the side of one hand into the palm of the other. "Kristin needs a plan. One that ensures Drew *never* recognizes her—"

"How about new hair?" Allie flipped her light brown ponytail. "Cut and color."

"No," Megan said. "He met her yesterday as a brunette

with her hair in an updo. New hair would be like putting a neon sign on her forehead blinking, *see me, see me, see me.*"

"Everyone would notice that change, not just Drew," Bree pointed out. "Kristin's hair would probably become a trending topic in the office."

"I love being discussed as if I'm not even here," I said over my shoulder.

"I think you need to just keep doing what you did yesterday." Megan's voice took on her courtroom tone, the one that influenced juries. "No makeup, hair pulled back, conservative clothing in neutral colors. Nothing to trigger any memories of the woman he met at breakfast."

The thought of keeping up the spinster librarian facade sent my heart into an anxious thrum. I liked color, and my wardrobe reflected it. "I don't think I have enough tan, cream, white, and black clothes for more than a few days of work," I said, frowning. "Hopefully I can pull together a few outfits that aren't totally out of style."

"No. Style is not your goal anymore," Megan said pointedly.

"Maybe wear the same outfit twice in the same week," Allie added.

"You want to be the woman he doesn't notice," Bree chimed in. "Earn a spot in the Glamour *Fashion Don'ts* column."

"Out-of-style should become my style?" The thought made me a little sick. "For the rest of the time I work at The Joneses, I have to dress...cluelessly?"

Bree gave me a sympathetic pat on the back.

That's when I realized I didn't have any other choice. I had to do whatever it took to keep my job. I couldn't afford to get fired. Sure, my parents were always willing to help me when I needed it, but I didn't want to go crawling home asking for money to tide me over...again.

"It's not forever," Megan said. "Rejuvenating The Joneses will take all his mental energy. Sooner or later Drew will forget all about that morning because the memory will be buried under lots of work-related details."

The retriever started barking at a dog across the park, and Allie tugged back on the leash to rein him in. "Megan's right. Drew's going to have more important things to worry about than some discussion he had at continental breakfast."

As the dog continued to strain against the leash, Allie sighed in resignation and sped up her pace. The beagle I was walking raced forward to make sure he wasn't left behind, forcing me to lengthen my stride too. Bree and Megan followed suit, and soon we were all jogging to keep up with the dogs.

"What if you're wrong about him forgetting? What happens if, despite everything, he recognizes me," I puffed out. "How do I explain why I didn't follow him to the donut shop? How do I explain why there isn't a review website called *Get out of Town*? How do I explain that I'm not really a reviewer without admitting everything I said that day was a lie?"

Allie opened her mouth to answer and I waved a hand to shut her down. "Drew Lawson is all about honesty. And this whole story is...not. So, what do I do?" I sucked in some air.

The other three looked at me as if I'd just announced that an alien spaceship was hovering overhead and wanted to know how we should defend ourselves.

"Stop." Allie commanded, and we instantly obeyed. Even the dogs.

We formed a circle on the path facing one another, breathing hard, each of us privately contemplating the scenario I'd just described. The dogs pranced impatiently across the grass, checking out all the new smells in the area.

Allie shook her head. "Based on what he said during his presentation, I'm afraid telling him the truth won't go well for you."

"You think?"

"There's a solution," Megan said in a deliberate voice. "You make the lie a truth."

We all swiveled toward her.

"You buy the domain GetOutofTown.com."

"What will that do?" I asked.

"You create a review website. Now you're not lying anymore."

A laugh burst out of me. "Oh yeah, I forgot I'm a programmer and making websites is all in a day's—"

"What's wrong with the dog?" Bree ran over to kneel

beside the retriever sitting in the grass holding his left paw in the air.

She peered at the bottom of his foot. "Oh, baby, you stepped on a bee!" She pulled a black and yellow bee from between the pads on his foot and tossed it to the ground. "He got stung by a bee!"

We gathered round the dog, patting and hugging and cooing out reassurance. After a minute, we set off again, moving slowly because the dog was limping, then coming to a complete halt when he sat and lifted his paw into the air, his brown eyes sad and confused.

"He's really hurting." I handed the beagle's leash to Bree and knelt beside the dog, the knees of my jeans wicking up the dew from the grass. "Let's just carry him back. Megan, can you help me?"

"He probably weighs more than seventy pounds."

"That's why we'll do it together. Come on, I'll lift his front."

"Oh, thanks so much saving his rear for me," she deadpanned.

On the count of three, we hoisted the dog into our arms, then began to take the path back to the shelter.

"He's heavy," Megan said.

"Think of it as a weight-lifting workout," Allie replied.

Megan gave a mirthless laugh. "I'll remind you of that when it's your turn."

"Okay, back to websites and domain names," Bree said, deftly changing the subject. "Kristin, there are sites where you can buy domain names really cheap. They also offer website templates. You just pick out a template, fill in the blanks, and you can have a website up and running in a few hours."

"Just like that." I would have snapped my fingers for emphasis but both of my arms were wrapped around the retriever and my muscles were already starting to burn. "Somehow, I don't think it's that easy."

"My students do it all the time—"

"That's because they grew up with a computer in one hand and a smartphone in the other. Kids these days are mini-programmers by the time they're ten."

"No, they're just used to being online. They know how to fill in the blanks."

"Fine, I get the template thing—" I shifted the dog to get a better hold, quickly concluding that Bree had been right; this dog definitely weighed more than seventy pounds. "But I have nothing to put in a template. A review website would need—dare I say it, a list of reviews. And photos, an About Us page, cross-links, maybe even a place for comments from readers." I tried to tamp down my rising alarm.

"Well, you do have that other option," Bree said. "If Drew recognizes you, just come clean and hope he's merciful."

Allie touched her forehead with two fingers. "Of course. Just explain to Mr. Integrity, Truthfulness, and Honor that you lied to him multiple times that morning, and that you were only stealing breakfast in an attempt to meet successful guys. I'm sure he'll understand."

"How about a blog site instead?" Megan asked, ignoring both of them. "Not a fancy website with cross-referenced reviews, a blog. You're just a blogger doing restaurant reviews. Much less complicated."

I took a few seconds to consider what she was saying. It sounded more doable, but... "There's still the problem of not having any reviews. Even if I write a couple this weekend, it won't be enough to make the site look legitimate."

"Kristin, you're in the Continental Breakfast Club now —we take care of our own." Megan grinned. "Why else would I be carrying the back end of a big, smelly dog?"

A lump leapt into my throat, and my eyes got watery. Her words were like a needle puncturing my panic balloon. I wasn't in this alone.

"You must not have read the bylaws," Allie said, nodding. "What it means is that, this weekend, we'll all be writing blog posts about restaurants for you to post on the site. By Sunday night, voila, instant credibility."

"Oh, I love you guys," I managed to get out. "I'm so glad I met you."

"We're glad we met you, too," Allie said.

Bree brought her hands together with a clap. "Okay, love fest is over. "What about pictures?"

"So easy." Megan circled her index finger in the air like she was wrapping up a video shoot. "We'll just drive over to the places we're writing about and take a few shots on our phones."

"One outside and one inside should be enough, don't you think?" Bree asked. "And no pictures of meals. Amateur food shots are always unappetizing."

Allie nodded. "Bad pictures won't help restaurants get new customers."

I shifted the dog in my arms to give my muscles a break. "Allie, remember, this isn't a real site."

"Once it goes live, it's real," Megan said. "You have to treat it that way."

Her words took me by surprise, but after a moment's reflection I realized she was right; I was about to open an online business.

"We're going to need a solid review of Grandad's Donuts," Megan said. "So if Drew ever goes to the site, he'll know you did what you promised."

Allie raised her hand. "I can check it out tomorrow morning."

"I'll go with you," I said. "If this ever blows up and Drew starts to ask questions, I want to have firsthand knowledge of Grandad's Donuts. It's okay if the other reviews are based on dinners we had months ago, but not this one."

"I agree. That review is the cornerstone," Megan said. "Once it's up, Drew won't have any reasons to have doubts about the site—or you."

Despite my concerns that the whole plan could go

south in a big way, excitement skittered over my skin. This could work. It could really work. I rubbed my nose in the fur of the retriever's neck, and he twisted his head to swipe a slobbering tongue across my mouth.

Hopefully that wasn't a sign of things to come.

Allie had plans with her boyfriend, Jax, that night. And Bree was going out with my brother, Adam, who she had been seeing ever since they met last month on Hatteras Island. That meant it was up to Megan and me to get the blog site started.

Right away Megan realized we shouldn't buy the domain name I had given to Drew: *Get Out of Town.* "If he Googled that name after you ditched him, he's already discovered there isn't a GetOutOfTown.com. We need to change it just enough that he thinks he got the name wrong." Megan pursed her lips, thinking. "How about GetOutaTown.com? Close to what you told him, but easy to misunderstand."

Bree and Allie always said she was brilliant. Now I knew it firsthand.

By ten p.m., after carry-out Chinese and a bottle of red wine, Megan and I had made big progress on my website. The header looked professional, the layout looked professional, my photo (that we'd taken on her phone half an hour earlier) looked professional.

With each passing minute, I was feeling more and more confident that Drew would never figure out this site was brand new and that I wasn't actually a reviewer. I know, desperation can make a believer out of anyone, but all I had to say was, thank God for website templates.

Early the next morning, I drove across the city to Grandad's Donuts, Allie riding shotgun next to me. The website said they opened at seven a.m. and we weren't much past that.

"There it is." Allie nodded at a storefront on the corner and pulled out her phone. "Slow down and I'll get a couple of pictures as we go by."

I rounded the corner to take a spin through the alley, on the lookout for a white panel van with a big pink frosted donut painted on each side. There were a couple of parking spots marked, *Reserved for Grandad's Donuts*, but the white van was nowhere in sight. "Hopefully, the van is out on deliveries—and the deliveryman isn't Drew," I said. "The last thing I need is for him to come back and spot me —the girl from breakfast, the girl from The Joneses—and start to ask questions."

"It makes no sense he'd be the driver," Allie said. "The regular guy must have been sick or on vacation or something. No way does the president of The Joneses have a part-time job delivering donuts."

Back on the street, I pulled into a parking spot, shut off my engine, and let my head fall back against the headrest, my heart pounding. What if I walked into the café and ran right into Drew? Everything would be over before it started. Maybe Allie should go in alone. Was it really so important that I tried more donuts? Was it really critical that I actually experience being inside the shop?

No, of course not. Not until the day Drew realized who I was and started asking questions. And then it would be massively important that my answers sounded legit. I pushed open my car door. "Let's go."

Inside the shop, the decor was pretty nondescript. The place had large windows overlooking the street, white painted walls, six café tables, and a big, glass display case full of donuts. The smell of fresh bakery wafted through the air, sweet and buttery, rich and fluffy. It was a good thing I didn't live nearby or I could see how Grandad's could become daily habit.

Oh, wait. Thanks to our new company president, it was already a daily habit at The Joneses. Suddenly my jeans felt too tight.

A man came out of the kitchen wiping his hands on the white chef's apron covering him from chest to knees. "Welcome to Grandad's. I'm Nate. Can I get you something?" A friendly smile lightened his face and crinkled the corners of his eyes.

I tried not to gawk. That smile, it was Drew's all the way. Were these two related? Brothers? Cousins? It explained everything—free donuts at The Joneses, Drew asking for a review to help the shop, him driving the delivery truck.

"Donuts," Allie chirped. "Those frosted ones with cherries on top look amazing!"

Nate slid open a glass panel at the back of the case. "Are these your first Grandad's Donuts?"

We both nodded. "What do you recommend?" I managed to get out.

He handed us a small menu that listed donut and coffee options on the front and a history of the business on the back. "They're all good. I don't put out a donut until I'm really happy with the recipe."

"So, you're the owner?" I asked, hoping to get some insight into Drew's connection to this place.

He nodded.

"And these are your own recipes?" Allie swept a hand across the display case.

"Most are mine. The fried cake and powdered sugar donuts are my great-grandfather's recipes. He ran a bakery."

"Hence the name," I said.

"Yeah. I took his basic recipes and started experimenting. Pretty soon, everyone was saying I should open a donut shop." He held up a finger and went back into the kitchen. "Hold on just a minute."

As soon as he was gone, I put my mouth close to Allie's

ear and whispered, "He could be Drew's brother. Big resemblance."

She jerked back and looked at me with wide eyes. I tilted my head and nodded firmly. Before we could even begin to theorize what this meant and how we could find out for sure, Nate returned with a plate holding two different donuts cut into quarters. "Try these. Fresh from the fryer."

I began to salivate. I'd already had Grandad's Donuts slightly warm; I could only imagine how delicious these would taste hot and fresh.

Allie popped a piece into her mouth and let out a soft moan. "Amazing," she murmured and immediately reached for another.

I nodded, unable to speak for the glorious flavors awakening my taste buds that fine Sunday morning.

The front door opened and a man came up to the counter to order a dozen donuts. Allie and I took the plate of donut quarters over to a table near the front window. We finished those babies off like we hadn't eaten in four days.

"These are so incredible," Allie whispered. "It's like I can't get enough."

"You see how I got in trouble at continental breakfast? Best donuts in the world."

Nate came over to our table once the customer was gone. "So what do you think?"

"These may be the best donuts in the world," Allie said.

He rubbed the bridge of his nose. "If I had a buck for every person who said that..."

He didn't need to finish his sentence; I already knew the rest. It had been six months and he couldn't get any traction. Grandad's Donuts was in trouble.

"Anyway, what can I get you two?"

We ordered two cappuccinos and six different donuts to share. "We can't make up our minds," I said, hoping it sounded like a reasonable explanation why we were about to seriously chow down on donuts.

As soon as Nate left to get our order, Allie pulled out her phone and stealthily took some pictures of the shop. "I'm thinking that, in order to do a really thorough review, we need to try every donut. Better yet, I might need to get a job here."

I wiped my fingers on a napkin. "You'll weigh five hundred pounds before the year is over."

"But I'll be so happy on my way up. I can't believe any place with donuts this good would be struggling."

"He's got the steak nailed, but he's got no sizzle."

"What?" Allie looked at me like I had a screw loose.

"Old advertising slogan. Sell the sizzle, not the steak. It means, focus on the experience, not the product. Appeal to the customer's emotions."

Nate set our order on the table and I waited until he was gone to continue. I broke off a piece of chocolate frosted donut and said in a low voice, "He needs to punch up his image. This room isn't very inviting. Would you want to hang out here with a friend?"

Allie pulled a face.

"Exactly. And the exterior...you can hardly tell it's a donut shop."

"But the donuts are so good."

"Right. Which goes to show you that success is about more than just offering a great product. You need to sell the sizzle."

"Maybe I should be selling more sizzle at Flawless Paws," Allie said about the dog grooming shop she owned. She took a bite of donut. "That is, if I don't close my doors and apply for a job here."

I smirked at her.

"Seriously, though, how would I sell the sizzle?" She sipped her cappuccino and eyed me expectantly.

"Off the top of my head...maybe you rename each service something cute. Like, a wash and cut is called The Marilyn Monroe."

"I don't get it."

"It's just an example."

"A bad one, I think."

"What do you want? On a normal Sunday, I would still be in bed right now." I took a swallow of cappuccino.

Allie shoved a chunk of cream-filled donut in her mouth and nodded as if to say, *Try again.*

I thought for a minute. "Okay, so you know that super

formal haircut for poodles where they end up with round balls of hair on their feet and the end of their tail? You rename that the Aristocut. Get it? *Aristocrat?* Aristocut?"

Allie was nodding along. "So what would you rename a flea and tick bath?"

Oh my God. I picked up a donut with fresh blueberries and raspberries pressed into a decadent caramel frosting, and took a big bite. "It's like this," I said around a mouthful of amazing flavor explosions. "He calls this one Caramel Berry. Ho-hum. That's a description, not the sizzle. Why not call it something interesting like, *Berry Delicious.*"

"Berry Delicious. That's cute. Or how about *Merry Berry* or *Merrily Berrily* or—" Allie waved an excited hand. "*Berrily we Roll Along?*"

I stared at her for a few seconds. "Right. He needs to make this place less typical, more fun." I took a donut off the plate. "This honey glazed is so good it should have a fitting name, something memorable—"

"How about *Sweet Talker?*" Allie lifted her hands. "Kind of a pun."

Nate came out of the kitchen with a large tray of fresh donuts, and I watched as he began to refill the display case. He was almost as handsome as Drew. Almost. But there was something about Drew that I found especially attractive—or I mean, I would have found especially attractive if he weren't my boss. "Better yet, how about *Sweet Lovin'.*"

Allie choked on her cappuccino. "Oooh, it would even

be fun to order. *Excuse me, but could I have some Sweeet Lovvvin'?*" She nudged a piece of donut sensuously into her mouth.

After finishing our donuts, we waddled to the display case to get some donuts for Megan and Bree who were already busy writing reviews. "How about two caramel berry, two chocolate cream cheese, and two butter almond," I said.

As Nate handed Allie the box, he said, "I threw in a couple of others for you to try. On the house."

"Wow, that's awesome. Thank you." Allie fixed her eyes on Nate for a long moment. Then she jerked her thumb in my direction and said, "My friend, here, has a great idea for you."

I turned stiffly toward him, my expression frozen. Our goal had been to get in here, eat some donuts, and get out.

"What's that?" Nate asked.

Allie flashed a grin my way. "Rename your donuts. Sell the sizzle, not the steak."

Nate's brows pulled together and I figured he was either confused or offended or both. Which was totally understandable. This business was his baby, and we'd just implied that he christened all his babies with stupid names.

I hastily described what selling the sizzle meant. "It's not that your donuts have bad names. They're just typical. Predictable," I said. "Your donuts are so much better than that—why not make sure people know they're getting something special."

I opened my hands, palm up. "Fun names make your donuts memorable. Memorable means people tell their friends." I pointed at the honey glazed donuts in the display case. "It's like this. You call that absolutely delectable, finger-licking delicious donut right there, *Honey Glazed.* I call it *Sweet Lovin'.*"

He started to laugh.

"No, seriously. Imagine when your customers tell their friends, *I got some Sweet Lovin' at Grandad's Donuts.* What do you think is going to happen next?"

"Everyone's coming to Grandad's for *Sweet Lovin'!*" Allie cried.

Suddenly I was caught up in the merits of convincing him he should give this a try. "Think if all your donuts had clever names—word couldn't help but spread. And word-of-mouth advertising is the best there is."

"Amen, sister!" Allie exclaimed.

Nate didn't say anything for several seconds. Then he nodded. "You might be on to something."

That was all the motivation I needed. Before I even had time to consider what I was doing, I was blabbering into new *save the world* territory. "Don't take this wrong," I said, stepping to the center of the room, "but you might consider some changes out here in the sitting area. It's not the kind of place that makes people want to linger. And what you want is to make people linger."

"I thought I wanted to sell donuts."

"You do. But there are many roads to Rome. You want the quick hitters—buy and leave. But you want the lingerers, too. The ones who buy and stick around, and then maybe buy some more. You want them to meet friends here for coffee and donuts. Maybe stick around to use the Wi-Fi."

He looked startled. "At a donut shop?"

"Absolutely." Allie nodded emphatically.

"You offer free Wi-Fi, right?" I asked.

"Not yet. That's bad, huh?"

"You have to offer Wi-Fi," Allie said.

"It's like a subliminal message to potential customers." I walked toward the front windows and pointed outside. "An unseen sign signaling *Welcome, Welcome, Welcome.*" I held up both hands, opening and closing my fingers like neon lights blinking on and off.

"So many people work from home. They stay inside the same four walls, alone, all day every day. Soon, they're longing for human contact, desperate for somewhere to go where they can work on a laptop for an hour or two and see other people, feel the flow of conversation going on around them, connect with the vibrancy of life."

Allie was nodding along like I was a motivational speaker at the pinnacle of my talk.

Nate contemplated his shop. "My brother thinks I need more tables."

"Your brother?" Allie asked without missing a beat. "Does he work here too?"

I held my breath.

"No. But he helps out once in a while. Does our deliveries if the regular driver can't make it, things like that."

"You definitely need more tables," I said in a rush as the air whooshed out of me. "And a bar-height counter with tall stools. It's perfect for people who are alone, or want to stand and work." My mind was spinning. The family connection had just been confirmed: Drew was Nate's brother. I tried to inhale before I passed out from lack of oxygen.

Nate was regarding me with a look of appreciation. "You seem to really understand this."

"I've spent a little time in coffee shops." I pulled out my wallet to pay for the donuts.

"You didn't learn all that drinking coffee." He waved away my credit card and reached out to shake my hand. "No charge. Your advice today is easily worth a few donuts. Thank you... I'm sorry, I don't think I got your name."

I bit my lip. He wanted my name? "Oh, uh—" Frantic thoughts began to ping-pong through my head. What if Nate mentioned this conversation to Drew? What if Drew figured out I worked at The Joneses? What if he realized I was the reviewer from continental breakfast? Would it matter? Why would it? Why wouldn't it? What consequences could there be? Think. Think. Think. There were so many moving parts, I couldn't keep them all straight. At this point, it was probably best if I didn't take any chances.

"I'm Kris—tine. Kristine... Carlotta," I said, slightly altering my first name and using my middle name as a surname to hide my identity.

I could hardly believe I was telling yet another lie. But better safe than sorry. One could never be too careful in these kinds of situations. Not that I'd ever been in a situation like this before. Okay fine, so that whole thing where I asked Bree to pretend to be my brother's girlfriend a few months ago on Hatteras Island came close, but these weird situations are not my norm. Really. They're not.

"Well, Kristine, thanks for your insight. I'm really glad you stopped in today."

As he reached out to shake Allie's hand, she said, "I'm Allie—" She glanced at me and I could tell her brain was whirring. "Allison Ann," she said, following my lead and using her middle name as her surname.

I almost choked holding back the laughter that wanted to escape out of me. Luckily, Nate didn't seem to notice our unusual names or my near convulsive reaction.

Allie and I were almost out the door when Nate stopped us with, "I have a question." We turned.

"Would you have any interest in helping me rename my donuts, and maybe putting together recommendations for changes inside here? Money's pretty tight right now, but I can pay you in donuts. For friends and family. All the donuts you can eat—or carry."

Allie and I exchanged a questioning frown.

Nate's mouth curved up in a hopeful smile. "I could really use...your help."

Well, what was I supposed to say to that? Come on, really, *what?*

"The best donuts in the world," Allie muttered.

The best, fucking donuts in the world. And a guy who needed saving. I was a goner. "Oh, well, okay, sure. Why not?"

And just like that, I was working for both brothers.

FIVE

That afternoon was gloomy and overcast, which was a relief because we spent it in my apartment on our computers, like students who had procrastinated writing their research papers until the day before they were due. It didn't take us long to realize that even though the name—Get Outa Town—implied this was a travel site, the United States was too big and we had too little time to cover the country.

For a few minutes we considered faking it by using restaurant and hotel pictures already online, then decided that might open us up to copyright issues. And the last thing I needed was to get embroiled in a lawsuit over stealing pictures because I didn't want my boss to find out I'd been stealing breakfast. Among other things.

I was starting to feel the weight of all those black marks on the whiteboard of my soul, as Sister Francesca, my second grade teacher, used to describe it. The past few weeks had probably changed my whiteboard into a blackboard.

Anyway, we reduced our review territory and Megan wrote an About Us page for the website that read like this: Get Outa Town is dedicated to helping you discover great places to eat and amazing places stay in and around Minneapolis. Our goal is to give you the information you need to plan your next getaway, night out, or adventure!

It took longer than we expected to put together each review because, invariably, we had to log onto each restaurant website to refresh our memories. And then we had to come up with unique things to say about each place so our reviews contained thoughtful evaluations of food, service, atmosphere, and décor—instead of sounding like cookie-cutter copies of one another.

"I need a break." Allie plopped back into her chair, then stood and crossed the room to the front window. "Every minute of this reinforces that I made the right decision by not going to vet school."

Bree joined her at the window. "Why don't you and I take a road trip to shoot some pictures before it gets any later? This dark cloud cover is already making the light bad for outside shots."

"Good idea," Megan said. "As soon as you finish each place, send the pix to my email so we can do cropping or color correction while you two are driving around."

The first three photos arrived an hour later.

"Not bad. A bit too dark," I said, leaning over Megan's shoulder to look at an exterior restaurant picture on her computer.

"I can fix that." Megan opened a photo editing software and began to make adjustments to the photo's brightness and contrast. Then she lightened the sky so it was no longer overcast. "I'm not hungry yet, but it won't be long," she said. "Should we have Allie and Bree to pick up some pizza on their way back?"

"I'll text them."

Bree's reply came in seconds later: Aren't you going to dinner at your grandma's?

I stood up ramrod straight and pulled back my sleeve to check at my watch. Shit. It was Sunday night. Family dinner at grandma's. Right about now, everyone was probably starting to sit down at the table. Normally, I could call and make an excuse; it wouldn't be an issue if I didn't go. But tonight we were celebrating my grandparents' anniversary. Even though Grandpa died eight years ago, Gram honored the date every year.

I texted back: Did Adam invite you?

My phone vibrated with her reply: *Yes, but I said I was busy.*

Getting out of dinner wouldn't be that easy for me. My thoughts raced. I couldn't miss the dinner. But I had to get this website up. I had to go to Grandma's. The website would save my job. The dinner. The website. But—but—

I squeezed my hands into fists at my sides, then slowly

opened my fingers. Grandma came first. She had to. This dinner was too important to her—and she was too important to me. "I have a problem," I said.

Megan glanced up from the computer.

"I'm really sorry. I have to go to my grandma's for a while. I totally forgot it's her anniversary dinner."

"I thought your grandpa—"

"He is." I shook my head. "That's why it's so important I be there. I can miss a lot of dinners, but not this one. I'll be back as soon as I can." I grabbed my purse and charged for the door. "I'll keep my phone next to me. If you need anything, just text."

Everyone was already at the table when I breathlessly burst through the door at Grandma's. I'd driven like such a maniac, I managed to cut ten minutes off the usual trip time. "Sorry, sorry," I said as I slipped into the empty seat between my mom and my brother, Ethan, and shoved my phone on the chair seat under my right thigh.

"We were getting worried that you forgot about tonight," Grandma said.

"No, no. I just lost track of— I'm working on a—project —and totally lost track of time."

My dad filled my wineglass with red wine and I took a quick sip.

"A project on Sunday. That's new. Does it have anything

to do with the changes at The Joneses? The new president?" Ethan handed me a big wooden serving bowl of tossed salad.

He had no idea how close to the truth he was. I didn't respond, just pretended to be fixated on using the tongs to put salad on my plate.

"Please note, everyone, the lack of a reply," my other brother, Adam, said with a mischievous grin. "One might surmise that *project* is actually code for, *Kristin has met someone.*"

Oh, yeah, I'd met someone all right. My worst possible nightmare. "Don't be dumb."

My phone vibrated, and I pulled it out to read a text from Megan: *What's the website password?*

I looked up to see everyone at the table watching me. I gave an apologetic shrug. "It's the project."

"The project sends text messages," Ethan said in an oh-I-believe-this kind of voice.

His wife, Heather tapped him on the arm. "Ethan."

I threw Heather a grateful look as I typed out a reply: *HoneyGlazed. All one word. Capital H, capital G.*

Shoving my phone under my leg again, I put a big helping of spaghetti and meatballs on my plate and took a quick taste. "This is amazing, Grandma."

"Your grandfather's favorite," she said, even though it was a well-known fact in the family. She took a bite of salad and watched me for a moment. "Are they finally giving you more responsibility at your job?" Her excitement sent a twinge of guilt through me.

"Sort of." My phone vibrated again and I scanned a new text from Megan: *HoneyGlazed not working.*

"Must be a pretty good prospect—oh sorry, *project*—if you're texting during the anniversary dinner," Adam added.

Really? Was my life going to be the entire topic of conversation tonight? I let out a quiet huff and texted a reply to Megan: *That's the right password. Do you have the right username? saveMe357.*

"What's the project about?" my dad asked.

"A guy," Ethan said like he was twelve years old. Then he and Adam laughed like they were eight.

"Give it a rest." I buttered a piece of Italian bread. "It has to do with a website."

"A new website?" my mom asked.

Oh shit, why did I say that? "It's the catalog site. We're creating a bigger digital presence." At her blank look, I added, "We're improving the website where we sell all the catalog stuff."

Grandma's eyes popped open. "You finally got your promotion!" She raised her wineglass. "Kristin got a new job!"

"You're in charge?" My mom clinked her glass against Grandma's.

"Hear, hear." "Congratulations!" "About time!" My dad, Ethan, and Adam said all at once.

I blanched. This was how rumors got started. I raised my glass and took a big swallow of wine because, obviously, I was going to need plenty of alcohol to get through this dinner. "It's not a promotion. I'm just helping out."

My phone vibrated again and I mentally groaned. Reluctantly, I read Megan's text: *What happened to admin357??*

"It could turn into a promotion as changes are made over there," Ethan said. "Didn't you say jobs may be on the line?"

I nodded without answering him. My fingers flew over the screen as I texted back: *You said admin would be too easy to hack, so I changed it. I told you...didn't I?*

Did I? Or were we so busy trying to get so much done so fast, I only thought I'd told her. I couldn't even remember.

A new text arrived from Megan: Too late. Tried log in 4 times with wrong info. System thinks I'm a hacker. Locked out.

"For God's sake," I muttered and texted back: *Can't you click a reset button?*

"What's the matter?" Heather asked at the same time my mom said, "Honey, is everything okay?"

I forced a smile. "Just a...glitch. You know, whatever can go wrong, usually does."

My phone buzzed and I quickly read the text: Tried to log in too many times. Can't reset now without tech support help.

Before I could even reply, a second text landed: It's Sunday night. Tech support closed. Opens 7am Pacific Time (9 our time). Can't help in morning—leaving town first thing to take deposition. No reviews on site.

My breath caught. I had an empty review site. I couldn't upload any reviews until the log-in data was reset. We all had to work tomorrow. And even if I called tech support from work as soon as they opened, I still wouldn't be able to upload any reviews until that night.

All the stress of the past few days cascaded like rain. Despair welled up inside me and I swallowed hard to hold back a sob.

Ethan put a hand on my arm. "You okay?"

I got more choked up.

"Don't worry. I'll kill the guy," he said.

"I'll help," Adam added.

I shook my head and gave them a lopsided grin. "Thanks for having my back, you guys, but this is something I have to work out myself."

By the time I crawled out of bed the next morning, I was exhausted from a fitful night's sleep. I showered and put my hair up in a knot and dressed in my new out-of-style style, sans makeup. After last night's disaster, I knew I had just one goal to accomplish today—avoid running into our new company president.

I was pretty confident I could do that. Since this was

only his second workday at *The Joneses*, his schedule had to be packed with important C-suite activities like reorganizing the company and making critical decisions. Chatting with low-level assistants shouldn't even make the bottom row of his first-week to-do list.

I delivered Carly's coffee exactly at eight, said good morning to Melanie and James, and managed to get to my workspace without seeing anyone else. Perfect. All I had to do was keep my head down, my voice quiet, my attention on my computer—and at exactly nine o'clock, I would call tech support. If I got this login fiasco taken care of right away, maybe I could take some of my lunch hour to upload a few reviews.

My office phone began to ring, and I picked up the receiver without bothering to check caller I.D.

"We have a meeting with the new president at ten," Carly said without a hello.

I gasped. "What?"

"Ten o'clock. To discuss the department and how we function. Make sure everyone knows, please." The fact she used the *please* word told me she was totally stressed about this.

"But why are we on the first day? I don't—"

"Use your head, Kristin. We develop the catalog's product mix. We're indispensable to the catalog's success—"

"So are the other departments!" I cried. "Why doesn't he meet with them first?"

There was a long pause. "To use an analogy," Carly said in a condescending voice. "Our department is the front row in the stadium. Just make sure everyone is there at ten." She hung up, and I sat there, unmoving, the receiver still gripped in my hand. How could this be happening? How could the simple wish to meet a single man turn into a race against time to hang onto my job?

Thank God I'd gone all out on spinster librarian style today. I was the perfect plain Jane. And, for the first time ever, I was grateful for Carly's overbearing personality. If there was one thing I could count on, she'd make sure I was virtually invisible in that meeting.

At ten o'clock sharp, the five people from our department were all seated around the big oval table in the conference room. Drew introduced himself as though we, somehow, didn't already know who he was. He was even better looking than on Friday—if that was even possible— and Melanie dropped her pen on the floor so she could have an excuse to bend in my direction as she retrieved it. "Hottie," she said under her breath on her way down.

Yeah, but the casual, donut cart guy we'd met on Friday was gone, and today Drew was all business. His demeanor was a stark reminder that jobs were on the line all over the company. I trained my eyes on the yellow pad of lined paper in front of me on the table and tried to contain my fear.

"What I'd first like to do is understand what everyone does here at The Joneses," Drew said in a crisp voice. "So, why don't each of you introduce yourself and take a couple of minutes to describe your job."

Talk? No, no, no. What I needed was a reason, any reason, to get out of this room before I had to open my mouth. Pneumonia might do it. No, I wouldn't even be at work with pneumonia. Sinus infection? Not bad enough. Food poisoning? My spirits began to rise. The mere mention of stomach cramps and diarrhea would be enough to make everyone insist I leave for the day.

"Would it help if I just ran through each person's responsibilities and activities?" Carly was sitting at the end of the table as though she'd called the meeting herself. "I've been with The Joneses ten years, so I have a thorough understanding of each position in the department. Knowing how busy you are, it might help speed things along."

Normally, I would be furious that she was trying to keep the spotlight on herself, but today I was overjoyed. If Carly did all the talking, I could just sit here quietly. No need to even draw attention to myself by mentioning food poisoning.

Drew shook his head. "Thanks, but I blocked off plenty of time. No need to rush." He turned to his left and asked Tracy, an older woman who worked in order fulfillment, to start things off. She was followed by Tom, who also worked in order fulfillment. Ten minutes later, we were back to Carly. She was sitting, posture perfect, serenely smiling as though trying to telegraph that this meeting was just the best thing ever.

"As you know, I'm Carly. Director of Merchandising."

I could practically hear the capital D and M in director and merchandising.

"Which means," she continued, "I play an integral role in choosing the product assortment that is ultimately featured in the catalog. I supervise the assistant buyers and the merchandising assistant—" She let her eyes light for a second on Melanie, James, and me, and I swear I felt the cold burn of ice. "—and coordinate with the production team to ensure each issue of the catalog achieves our marketing goals and objectives."

As she settled into her *I'm-so-important* mode of speaking, I mentally prepared to be publicly shoved down the rungs of the same ladder she was climbing. Happened anytime someone of importance came around. Typical Carly.

"My goal," she said as though she alone ran the place, "is to feature unique items that give the more affluent members of our society the assurance that they have *arrived,* as well as feed their important need to project a successful image. Sometimes I employ the use of focus groups. Other times, I conduct one-on-one interviews to gain insight into what those affluent members value, what they feel might be lacking in their lives, and how The Joneses can fulfill those needs."

She ran a hand over her pad of paper as though

perusing notes she'd jotted down, but I knew it was all for show. When you've seen the act as often as I have, you recognize it immediately. Every word she was speaking had, no doubt, been carefully crafted and relegated to memory over the weekend.

Carly nodded at Drew as she droned on, describing everything she did in the greatest detail, including how it benefited the company. Funny how there was no mention of the three of us—James, Melanie, and me—who were basically the wind beneath her damn wings.

"What I think would be helpful," she said in a honeyed voice, "is for you and me to meet one-on-one. I couldn't resist checking out your past, and I see you've been involved in helping more than a few companies rise to new levels of success from the financial side. I think your thoughts would be extremely beneficial as I work on the product mix for the next edition."

Suck. Up. I glanced at Melanie and she pressed a finger against her chin, our secret sign for gagging...a useful substitute when it's not publicly acceptable to stick a finger in one's mouth and pretend to vomit.

Carly inspired many a finger pressed to the chin.

Drew nodded. "Once I'm done with the departmental interviews, we can set something up."

In quick succession James and Melanie described their roles as assistant buyers. Then it was my turn.

"I'm Kristin, the merchandising assistant. I support the buying staff," I said in the same throaty voice I used last

Friday. "I track and organize samples." I'd read over my job description that morning to make sure I used the best words to describe my responsibilities. Maybe if I could impress this guy even a bit he'd see my potential, and when Carly was finally named vice president, a new job would open up for me, too. "I also ensure product quality assurance, create purchase orders, and oversee shipping timelines."

Carly leaned forward to interject, "Kristin provides excellent ground-level support by maintaining our product files. She's our eager-beaver Girl Friday."

See what she did? *Ground-level.* I just skidded all the way down the ladder to land with a thud in the dirt. Drew probably thought Carly was giving me a compliment.

James threw me a sympathetic frown, and Melanie pressed her finger so hard into her chin she left a red mark behind.

Drew smiled at me longer than necessary. Heat prickled my skin. Did he recognize me? Or was he just pleased to hear I was such a good little worker?

"Can't put out a catalog of this magnitude without a team that supports each other," he said, catching my eyes with his.

I examined the table top, disconcerted by his attention.

"This department is so integral to the catalog, I want to bring you up to speed on the vision and direction chosen by the board." Drew steepled his fingers. "We've done an in-depth analysis of where the catalog began, where it is now, and where it's headed."

I slanted a sideways look at Melanie. We'd discussed this many times ourselves.

"As you all know, the catalog was originally geared toward a select market—the extremely wealthy. It offered unusual, expensive items that couldn't be found anywhere else. Over time, however, in a quest to reach an even broader market, the product mix became diluted. On top of that, the rise of the Internet made it easier for people to find our unique products elsewhere. Once goods featured in The Joneses were no longer viewed as exclusive, The Joneses ceased to be a destination for those people seeking items that...set them apart, shall we say. Which, logically resulted in declining sales."

Drew pushed a copy of the catalog across the table toward Carly. "So we're going back. To the original vision for The Joneses—appealing to that extremely wealthy market by creating a more *robust* merchandise mix."

Robust? Oh, great, he was one of those guys into business jargon.

"I've gone through the catalog and crossed out the products that can readily be found at other retailers—or just don't fit the image we want to convey."

Carly began to coolly flip the pages, her only reaction an occasional flicker of the eyelids. And then, as if aware she was telegraphing her disapproval, she shuttered that response behind her usual steely front. I was tempted to bend sideways to see what had been eliminated, but figured I'd find out soon enough.

"What I'll need are suggestions for replacement items," Drew said as Carly continued to whip through the pages. "Unique, expensive products not easily found elsewhere. And this is very time-sensitive. I'll need those ideas quickly, in a day or two."

Carly closed the catalog and fixed a calm gaze on him, her eyes slightly narrowed. He didn't know her well enough to realize she was furious. But the rest of us did. Carly was fully vested in this catalog mix. As she had proudly mentioned earlier, she had personally chosen many of the items. So, in her mind, Drew had just announced that her selection sucked.

Melanie cast an amused look my way, and I pressed my lips together to hold in a laugh.

"As my dad mentioned on Friday, we'll also be expanding our digital presence. The Joneses online store needs to be bigger and better. More user friendly. We're interviewing digital firms to redesign the website and provide SEO—search engine optimization. Our goal is to make the site a destination for people with some time to kill and a great deal of disposable income to spend. I'll have more on that later, once we choose a firm and sign a contract." He glanced around the table. "Any questions?"

We shook our heads in silent unison.

"I'll start researching replacement items," Carly said.

Drew tipped his head at me, James, and Melanie. "Our

worst enemy right now is time. We need to pull this catalog out of the fire quickly. So it's important to have as many eyes on it as possible."

Oooh, Carly was not going to like that. As if our next move had been choreographed, James, Melanie and I spun toward Carly to see her reaction.

"Typically, the most efficient method has been for me to source the items and work up the proposals." Carly raised her chin as if to impress upon Drew that she knew exactly how to handle this. "My team...serves as a backbone for me, with responsibilities in line with their experience levels."

Her words delivered a slow burn. Those of us who were *her backbone* did all the research to find the new products. Then she chose the items she liked best, after which her *backbone* created a presentation deck for her to show management in a meeting to which we were never invited.

We did the work, she got the glory.

"I'm confident you'll be very pleased with what I come up with. Previous management always was. I can have a presentation ready for you next week," she said, sliding back her chair as though the discussion was over.

Drew stood. So did Carly. He reached out to shake her hand.

My mouth wanted to fall open. I couldn't believe C.B. had pushed back against the new president—and won.

"I think you misunderstood," Drew said. "Two days.

We're on a tight schedule. If you don't think you can meet that deadline—" His eyes flicked over James and Melanie before coming to rest on me again. What? *What?* I froze, not even blinking. "—maybe one of your assistants can take it on."

Carly's expression hardened with restrained fury. "Two days is no problem at all."

"Good. Let's make it happen, *team,*" he said before striding from the room.

Melanie wasted no time spreading the word that Carly, the golden girl, had been put in her place by the new president. Depending on each person's position in the company, the news was either a chill wind or a welcome breeze. For the first time in a long time, my job felt a little exciting, like there might be a place for me to grow under this new management.

Well, as long as this new management didn't discover the truth about me and continental breakfast.

"You're not going to believe what Nicole told me now," Melanie said in a stage whisper as she rounded the corner into my work area. "Human resources met with Drew first thing this morning, and they all had to do the same thing we did—describe what they do. So apparently, the director was reading his job description off a sheet of paper like a robot, and Drew told him to put it aside and just use his own words to describe what he does.”

“Doesn't he just surf the Net all day?” I said with a chortle.

“So I hear. Nicole said he stammered around, and finally came out with some vague statement about overseeing a broad range of activities to ensure the company's success. To which Drew replied, Since the company isn't succeeding, I guess we can blame it on you.”

I almost spewed out my mouthful of coffee. “No way.”

Melanie grinned and nodded. “Not only is this Drew guy gorgeous, he's smart. It's going to be great having this hottie at the helm, don't you think?”

Yeah, if only I wasn't dragging a steamer trunk full of donut baggage behind me. I had a ways to go before I could relax with Drew running the company. I picked a piece of lint off my skirt.

“Admit it, you loved seeing someone give Carly a slap on the wrist in the meeting this morning,” Melanie said. “This could be awesome. Think about it...if there's a shakeup and they need to fill positions, maybe you could get a new job.” She spun and curtsied like she had just finished up a dance recital. “Maybe we both could.”

“This isn't a new line of thought for me,” I said. But it definitely was a reminder that I had to cover my ass and get those reviews uploaded to *GetOutaTown.com* as soon as possible.

Melanie put her hands on my desktop and bent toward me. "There are opportunities ahead, I feel it."

"We just have to make ourselves unforgettable and irreplaceable," I said, repeating her oft-repeated mantra. "You know, that thought just came to me—I don't know from where. Maybe it was a message from a higher power or something."

"Very funny. This is serious, Kristin."

Oh, if she only knew how serious it really was.

Melanie fixed a somber gaze on me. "So, I have to ask... is *unforgettable* the reason you've got this new style going on? Are you trying to look like successful, rich people who don't care about...fashion? Because I have to tell you, most wealthy people do care about style. It's only the eccentric oddballs who keep dressing in clothes they've pulled from the back of their closet and wearing their hair in a style from another era."

I pretended not to know what she was talking about.

"Come on, Kristin, suddenly you're only wearing beige, gray, and black. Your hair is wound in such a tight topknot your eyes seem perpetually surprised, like you've had bad plastic surgery. And you're wearing no makeup. Not even mascara. This is not you. So spill it. What's going on?"

Damn. I'd been able to deflect her questions last Friday by lying about feeling sick. What excuse could I make today? And tomorrow? And next week? And the week after that?

"Just, um, doing a test," I said, wondering where my

mouth was taking me because my brain was totally not in control at that moment. "Last Friday, when I wasn't feeling so well, I had an idea. To, ah, test—" Oh, what the hell was I testing? Why hadn't I just said I was tired of wearing makeup and that a colorful wardrobe was just so last year, or something?

Melanie nodded, waiting.

"Well, to see if people take me more seriously when I'm...not as attractive."

She started to laugh. "Not as attractive. Honey, you've left *not-as-attractive* behind and veered right into *dowdy*."

Dowdy? This is what I'd come to? Dowdy? I tried to gamely bury my mortification beneath pragmatism. If dowdy kept Drew from recognizing me, then dowdy was worth it. I couldn't afford to lose this job. "I like to think of it as conservative classy."

I started rearranging the bright push pins on my cubicle wall into a circle. "It's great, by the way, not to have to do my hair and makeup every morning. I get to sleep a half hour later."

Kristin rolled her eyes at me. "Sorry, you're not convincing me."

"Convincing you of what?" James stopped in the doorway, and Melanie and I both gave a start.

"To, quit wearing makeup and—"

"Dress like an old lady?" James interjected.

"What?" I asked, shocked. Did I look that bad? I mentally stomped on my dismay. "I'm thinking of the boardroom," I said defensively. "Will I get there faster if my appearance shows I'm focused totally on my work—instead of on my appearance?"

James considered my words for a moment, then gave his head a shake. "My guess? No. Think about all those business slogans. Dress for success. Have a can-do attitude. Fake it until you make it. It's not what you say, it's how you say it. Act like you belong in the boardroom and you'll find yourself there eventually."

"Wow, James. And your point is?" Melanie asked.

"It's simple. To get ahead, you have dress like you belong. And act like you belong."

Reminded me of Megan's advice for sneaking into continental breakfast: *Act like you belong, and you belong.* Pretty much the same thing.

I began to mull over how this advice might relate to my career trajectory. Had I ever acted like I belonged in the boardroom? Get real, was that a trick question? Of course I hadn't. It never occurred to me to act like I belonged in the boardroom. First of all, the boardroom is on a different floor. But second, it would have been hard to act like I belonged in the boardroom when I was picking up Carly's dry cleaning.

Just saying.

"So, what did you two think about today's meeting?" James glanced between Melanie and me. "Think our beloved CB is on the firing short list?"

"Who knows? She didn't put herself on Drew's new best friend list, that's for sure," Melanie replied.

My desk phone rang; Caller ID told me it was the boss. "Quiet. It's the woman herself." I lifted the phone to my ear and chirped, "Hi Carly."

"Kristin! I need you to find Melanie and James and come into my office. Immediately," Carly's no-nonsense voice clipped through the receiver. "We need to strategize."

I pulled a face. "Okay, I'll find th—" I began, but she'd already hung up.

I gave Melanie and James a patently fake smile. "Carly wanted to know if the three of us have some any extra time in our schedules. And if so, could we please stop in her office and help her work up some ideas to show Drew. Whenever it's most convenient, of course."

James chuckled. "In other words, get the hell in here right now or heads will roll."

"Close enough."

SIX

OUR STRATEGY MEETING WAS WINDING DOWN, THE CLOCK marching toward noon, and my stomach rumbling. I studied the dish of mini candy bars on Carly's desk and tried to figure out how I could take one without her noticing. You might wonder why I didn't just help myself. It was because the candy was there for show. Carly never ate any, we weren't allowed to touch them; only management could help themselves to the candy on her desk.

I'm not proud to admit this, but sometimes when she was gone, Melanie, James, and I would sneak in and help ourselves. James was the worst. Then we would cover our tracks by preemptively telling her a vice president or a director had been on the floor for a meeting. Worked every time.

"I've gone over the supplier lists and determined who

should reach out to which vendor. I'll email each of you a list once we finish up here," Carly said, her manner even more intense than usual. "If I'm going to make a killer presentation in two days, I'm going to need options from each of you tomorrow so there's time for me to choose the product mix and have the presentation deck created. Clear your schedules for the rest of today and tomorrow because, as Drew pointed out, time is of the essence. I suggest lunch might be best spent at your computers. And we'll all need to work late tonight." She paused. "I suspect that with the ambitious calendar Drew is putting together, we'll all be working the weekend as well."

Pressure began to build behind my ribcage. My job needed a ton of hours out of me today. But in the middle of all that, somehow, I needed to call tech support and reset the password on GetOutaTown.com. I needed to upload the reviews so I would be protected if Drew ever recognized me. The thought gave me pause. The question wasn't *if*, it was *when.* Sooner or later, Drew would realize we'd met before. Which meant, I had to reach tech support as soon as possible. Because, the way my life was going, if I waited until late tonight to call, without a doubt, tech support would have burned down.

"Kristin?"

I blinked and focused on Carly. "Yes?"

She apparently expected an answer about something. "You're on board with working late tonight, correct?"

"I can for a little, but ah, I've got...a dentist

appointment at...six," I said, wondering if dentists even worked that late.

"Cancel it."

"I won't be able to get back in for months and, uh, I think I have a cavity."

Carly's eyes narrowed. "You only have to wait to reschedule a cleaning. If you have an actual problem, they'll squeeze you in right away."

The blood pounded in my ears. Of course she was right. "How about if I work later tonight. At home."

"That goes without saying." Carly's lips tightened into a straight line as she considered James and Melanie, then came back to me as if she were trying to decide which of us should be tossed into a pond of alligators first. She touched a finger to her lips. "That gives me an idea. Let's brainstorm this a minute. Maybe there's something at the dental office we could put in the catalog, things the average wealthy person might not already have."

James made a choking sound. "Like what? A drill? Buy your own dentist's drill? Work on your own teeth?"

I gaped at him.

"Blasphemy," Melanie murmured for my ears only.

"Don't be absurd," Carly snapped. "Of course not a drill. I have no idea what might be there, but we need to show Drew we're up to the challenge with fresh ideas outside the box."

"How about a school of piranhas in a giant aquarium?" I deadpanned, emboldened by James.

"That's exactly what I'm talking about." Carly straightened her back. "A wall-size fish tank filled with exotic fish. And by wall-size, I mean ten feet or more."

Oh my God.

James opened and closed his mouth like a piranha biting into its prey, but Carly didn't even notice because she was too busy pointing her index finger at me like a gun. "Reschedule your appointment. Then look into what wall-size aquariums cost. And while you're at it, check out wall-size terrariums. This is the kind of thinking we need to make an impression on Drew."

Wall-size terrariums? From the corner of my eye I could see Melanie looking at me, but I knew I couldn't meet her gaze or I'd explode in laughter.

"I'm on it," I said with a hearty dose of enthusiasm so I sounded like a team player. But seriously, who wants a giant terrarium? Although, maybe the reason I don't understand the appeal is because my income is missing, like, seven zeros at the end. But honestly, even if I were stinking rich, I wouldn't want a terrarium wall. Especially if it had a lizard living in it.

Carly clapped her hands together twice like she was a quarterback ending a pep talk in the huddle. "Okay, people, let's make it happen," she said, repeating Drew's words from this morning. She tapped a finger on her watch. "I have to run an errand at noon, but I'll be back as soon as possible."

As we stood, I could see Melanie's index finger

twitching like she had to forcibly hold it back from flying up to push itself into her chin.

"Short list," I whispered as we went into the hall. "Pray there really is a short list and she's on it."

"Pray more that we're unforgettable and irreplaceable," Melanie muttered. "Because C.B. seems ready to pop."

I nodded agreement. The truth was, I didn't think I'd ever seen Carly wound quite so tight. And I'd never heard her say she was going to work late. Obviously, for all her smug bluster, she was feeling the same pressure as the rest of us—jobs were truly on the line.

Back at my desk, I pulled a bag lunch from my bottom drawer while I stabbed a finger onto my keyboard to rouse my computer from sleep mode. An email opened from Carly: Attached is your list of vendors to contact. We need to give this 200%. Let's take it to the next level and find products that provide maximum impact and deliver a successful future for all of us. C.

Did she actually think I believed she cared even an iota about saving my job? I let out a snort. Carly was just so... Carly.

Before I even started contacting vendors, I had another job-saving measure to complete: resetting the Get Outa Town login credentials. I got through to tech support right away and a techie fixed the problem in seconds. He even insisted I log in while he was on the line to make sure everything worked right, which it did.

I gave in to my unadulterated joy and pushed off the

floor with both feet to send my chair clunking through a lopsided spin. My cellphone buzzed from my desktop and I snagged it as I spun into a second rotation, expecting to find a text from one of the girls asking how things were going...and whether I'd managed to stay out of Drew's line of sight. I swiped the message open and read: *Taking part in Taste of Twin Cities weekend after next. Any chance we can get the donuts renamed this week? No pressure. Nate*

I rammed my feet against the floor, stopping my chair like a merry-go-round run aground. My to-do list had just escalated from urgent to emergency. I had The Joneses product proposals to come up with. My website needed reviews. And Nate wanted donut names. I put both hands over my sternum and exhaled slowly to control my nerves.

Prioritize. Make a list. Decide what was most critical and do that first. Get something done and cross it off. That was the only way I'd be able to keep myself from freaking out with so much going on.

I dashed off a reply to Nate saying Allie and I had already begun working on donut names (we had, if you counted our brainstorming in his shop yesterday) and would have something for him soon. Then I let myself dream about how it would feel to have the website done and my life back to the way it had been BCB, *Before Continental Breakfast*. The product proposals and donut names would feel like a walk in the park once I no longer had to worry about Drew recognizing me.

The temptation to eliminate that stress was so great, it

took major willpower for me to put my energy toward finding new products instead of immediately uploading reviews to the website. Munching on the peanut butter sandwich I'd packed for myself that morning, I began visiting vendor websites, running searches, and printing information sheets about products to investigate further. I did my best to stay centered, but my thoughts kept going back to the reviews—and the email Megan had sent describing how easy it was to upload them.

I sat back in my chair. It would be such a relief to get it done; maybe I should just go for it. As long as Carly was out, I'd be okay. I took a quick walk past her office to confirm she was gone, logged into Get Outa Town, then perused the list of completed reviews in my inbox.

Blue Caboose Café would be my test upload.

I typed the headline we'd written last night, *Choo Choo through an Amazing Meal,* into the proper spot, uploaded the review and photos per Megan's instructions, then opened a new window to view the live site. The Get Outa Town homepage opened with the review for Blue Caboose Café front and center. I let out a soundless squeal and whispered, "I love you" about a thousand times.

I quickly uploaded the Grandad's Donuts review and two others, checking the live site after each one to make sure everything was working right. One more review would make it five and then I'd quit. My fingers flew over the keyboard as I added the headline: *Nicatelli's Pizza Delivers a Breezy Cheesy Pizzee Pie.*

Corny. I cringed as I clicked *save* and switched over to the live site for final inspection. Happiness filled me. The site looked so real, I doubted anyone would ever question its authenticity. I crossed my arms over my chest and stared at the screen proudly. We had pulled it off.

"How's the research coming?"

My heart flipped, and I watched as Carly stepped to my desk and began to flip through the product sheets lying there.

"I've found some interesting items," I managed to get out, gesturing at the pages she was holding. "Still gathering information."

My mouse finger itched to minimize the windows I had open on my screen, all related to Get Outa Town, but I was afraid to move for fear Carly would notice and think I was trying to hide something.

"Hmmm. Might be some potential here. Send me the links and info as soon as you have all the details." She tossed the sheets back onto my desk and gestured at my computer screen. "And this? What is this?"

"It's a review site."

Her brows pulled together as she bent to peer at the screen. "Get Outa Town?" she said with a little sniff. "It doesn't sound like it would appeal to our target audience, Kristin. Improper English and all."

I squeezed my left hand into a fist on my lap. "You're probably right." With three quick clicks, I exited all the open windows.

"If you ever expect to make it beyond merchandising assistant, you're going to have to be able to recognize small things like that." Carly gave me wan smile, then spun on her stilettos and strode from my workspace.

I grabbed the top sheet of paper off my desk and crumpled it into a ball. Pulling my arm back, I took aim at the back of her head, a stream of curse words hanging on the tip of my tongue. For once, I was going to—

Going to what? Just what did I plan to do? Clearly, I was losing it.

I dropped my arm and smoothed open the wadded paper. Then I picked up my phone and started calling vendors to put bugs in their collective ears about needing new product ideas immediately. In between calls, I ran one Internet search after another, on a quest for out-of-the-norm stuff that was ultra-expensive.

Working feverishly, I bookmarked the website of a company that makes a computer-controlled showerhead with sixteen body zones that can be independently set for temperature and pressure (from misting rain to powerful jets), controls for a range of mood lighting and light shows, and a scent infuser. All for just fifty thousand dollars. Then I bookmarked the page for a diamond massage, provided in the comfort of your home for six hundred dollars (probably not expensive enough for the new catalog, but worth mentioning anyway). If you've never heard of a diamond massage, you're probably in the wrong income bracket. It's an anti-aging, detoxifying treatment that involves exfoliating the client's body with diamond dust cream then removing it with magnetically-enhanced gloves to eliminate the effects of electromagnetic pollution and stress.

I guess the rich really are different from the rest of us.

I found slippers studded with real rubies for a cool three million. A hot tub boat that lets you float in the middle of a lake and be in a hot tub at the same time, just fifty thousand. A whale-shaped, two-person submarine for a mere hundred thousand. A ten foot tall peacock composed entirely of seasonal plantings—just sixty-five grand. And a two-week getaway on a private island for only two hundred thousand.

It was all so...over the top. Did people really need this kind of stuff? *How much was enough?* I slapped the thought into the dark recesses of my mind and locked it away. It wasn't up to me to question the catalog's direction; I just had to do my job.

By mid-afternoon, my neck was killing me from hunching over the computer for so long. And I was starving again. The lunch I'd brought—and devoured hours ago—had been sparse because my refrigerator had been empty because I'd spent all weekend building a website and writing reviews instead of hitting the grocery store. Rubbing the back of my neck, I headed for the stairwell.

"Poverty break?" Melanie asked, using the play on words we liked to make on the phrase, *potty break.*

I gave a wry laugh. "Need just a few minutes to reacquaint myself with what really matters—at least to me."

It was fascinating to work at The Joneses, to see the kind of stuff rich people spent their money on. But I'm not going to lie, sometimes it was depressing to know that there were people who spent more money on a peacock made out of flowers for their backyard than I made in a whole year.

I took the stairs to the third floor, then opened the door to the stairwell that led to the roof. The moment the warm sun hit my skin and the breeze tried to pull my hair from its oh-so-tight knot, I began to relax. It wasn't fancy up there, just a couple of old semi-rusted, black wrought-iron tables and chairs off to one side, and a couple of neglected potted plants.

Most people who worked in the building didn't even know you could come up here, and probably wouldn't bother even if they did. It was a lot easier to walk outside to the picnic tables set up under a copse of maple trees near the warehouse entrance.

I liked the roof, though, for what it gave me—a better view, some privacy, and a place to grow vegetables, something I couldn't do at my apartment. Crossing the roof to the sunniest corner, I knelt beside a row of rectangular pots holding my plants: tomatoes, pole beans, green peppers, leaf lettuce, carrots...and weeds. Lots of weeds.

"You guys are beautiful." I ran my hands over the lush plants and inhaled the earthy scent of greenery and dirt. "Who needs a million dollar crystal piano when you can have these delicacies?"

I picked a couple of ripe cherry tomatoes and popped them into my mouth. The homegrown flavor burst over me; you couldn't buy a tomato in the store that tasted this good. I pulled a green pepper off the plant, ate it like an apple, then helped myself to another handful of tomatoes.

This felt so much more real than a diamond-studded dog collar that cost more than some people spent on a house. I shoved a finger into the dirt, dry and hard from the hot days and lack of rain. I hadn't been up to water my plants nearly enough lately; it was good to see they weren't wilting. I reached for one of the two plastic milk jugs filled with water that I stored behind the pots.

"Stuff is not the answer," I lectured the lettuce as I poured water over it. "Especially not super-expensive, show-off stuff. Although I admit, I can see how making more money might come in super handy."

I emptied both gallons over my potted garden, frowning as the dirt sucked up the moisture and still looked desert-like afterward. When in hell was it going to rain? As I recapped the empty jugs, tension began to rear its head again. My list had just gotten longer.

My garden needed watering and weeding. Drew needed unique product ideas. Nate needed new donut names. Get Outa Town needed more reviews. And everything needed to happen yesterday. "Breathe, just breathe. Take one thing at a time," I said, talking myself off the ledge once again.

Refilling the jugs and watering the plants would take ten minutes, max. I could do that right before I went home tonight—once I'd finished the product searches. If I stayed up here five minutes more, I could even pull the weeds, harvest the ripe tomatoes, peppers and beans, and even cut some lettuce. After that, I'd head home and upload the rest of the reviews. And then I'd come up with new donut names for Nate.

Okay, I had a plan. As long as I didn't try to fit in some sleep, everything would work out just fine.

By seven o'clock, I had reached the point of diminishing returns. Businesses on the East Coast and in the Midwest had been closed for hours, the West Coast was at the end of its day, and there really wasn't anyone left for me to call. I ran a few more Internet searches, said goodnight to Melanie and James, then swung past Carly's office to tell her I'd done all I could for the day.

That's when I discovered she had already left.

Her office was dark, the desk neatly arranged. I put my hand on the metal shade of her desk lamp to see if it still held any heat. No. I reached underneath to touch the lightbulb. Not even lukewarm. She'd been gone for a while. Apparently, the comment about putting in a two hundred percent effort only applied to Melanie, James, me.

I scooped three mini-Snickers from the candy dish on her desk and devoured them on my way up to the roof to take care of my garden. After refilling the empty jugs in the third floor restroom, I emptied the contents over my garden, then knelt to clean out the weeds. My stomach grumbled loudly as if chastising me for not taking more candy from Carly's desk, and I shoved a few cherry tomatoes into my mouth. Tomato juice dribbled down my chin and onto my white shirt. "Dammit," I muttered, swiping at the mess to keep it from absorbing into the fabric, and instead, adding a strip of mud across the spreading red stain.

"Fuck," I said loudly. "Fucky, fuck, fuck, fuck fuck."

"I've heard talking to plants makes them grow," a voice said from behind me. "Does talking dirty make them more fruitful?"

My heart skipped a beat. Two beats. Three. I couldn't breathe.

I glanced over my shoulder toward the voice I prayed didn't belong to Drew Lawson.

Prayer didn't work. Drew stood about six feet behind me, grinning.

This was like déjà vu. How had I missed seeing him...again?

SEVEN

"Sorry. Didn't know anyone was up here." I tried to seem unfazed as I stood and brushed off my hands, acutely aware of the muddy tomato stain highlighting the left side of my shirt.

Where had he come from? How could I not have noticed? Okay, sure, I was in a hurry, really focused on taking care of plant business and going home. And it wasn't like I'd inspected the entire rooftop when I got up here, but come on, I hadn't even heard so much as a footstep.

"I'm just exploring." Drew stretched his shoulders. His shirt sleeves were cuffed up a couple of times exposing tanned forearms. "The cleaning guy said there were tables up here and I thought I'd take a look. Just needed a break."

Chitchatting with Drew for too long could only be a recipe for disaster, but I didn't want to take off too fast and come across as rude. I needed to maintain the kind of cool head it would take to balance on a wire stretched between two skyscrapers. "Pretty busy, huh?"

That inane comment is what my cool head delivered?

"That's an understatement." He started to yawn, then stopped himself. "Is this is your garden or...is it a Joneses thing?"

"Mine. It's mine. Hardly anyone ever comes up here, so I thought, well..." I opened both hands palm up. "Why not grow some tomatoes?"

He nodded at the four big pots. "Tomatoes and then some."

I shifted nervously. I'd never asked for permission to grow anything up here. "Tomatoes did so well, I sort of expanded. This is probably my limit, though."

"Are those peppers?"

"Yeah. And lettuce, beans, and carrots," I said, pointing to each in turn. I couldn't believe I was making small talk about vegetable plants with the company president.

"Any corn?"

"Not a good container plant. It doesn't yield much when you grow it in pots." I had to get out of here. I had forgotten to use my breathy voice, so now there was even more chance he might recognize me from continental breakfast.

Drew leaned forward to peer at the plants, then pointed at a couple of big weeds. "What's that? And that?"

I grabbed one in each hand and pulled them out. "Weeds."

"Weeds?" he asked in mock dismay. "You mean I failed to identify something of nutritional value?"

He was so self-deprecating, I couldn't help but grin. Our eyes met. Warmth tiptoed from my heart to my nether regions, and I quickly pretended to inspect my garden. "If it makes you feel any better, my garden is in pretty rough shape. There are so many weeds, it's hard to see what I planted. I was just cleaning it up..."

"And I stopped you. Go ahead, I've got to get back to work anyway," he said, but he didn't leave.

Oh God, this was so awkward. I squatted down and began to clear out the weeds in the end pot. My movements were stiff, like I was a first-time guest on a garden show and the director had instructed me to just act naturally. Like that would be even remotely possible with the cameras rolling—or Drew Lawson watching.

As I methodically cleared out the weeds, three rows of carrots appeared like magic. I didn't have to look up to know Drew was still there. "These are Scarlet Nantes," I said to fill the silence. "They're originally from France." I pulled one out of the soil and held it toward him. "Try it."

"Dirt and all?"

"I take it you've never had a garden."

"My vegetables come from the store, already cleaned and cut up."

Of course they did. What did I expect? This guy just

took over a catalog that catered to the very rich. I tipped my head and continued weeding. A moment later I heard a crunch and glanced up to see him holding the carrot with the end bitten off. A smudge of dirt marred the right leg of his khakis where he'd obviously wiped off the carrot. I held back a smile.

"It's sweet," he said around the mouthful of carrot.

"Now you know why I'm growing my own." I plucked a couple of cherry tomatoes and handed them up to him. "These are Matt's Wild Cherry tomatoes." What the hell, I might as well go full-on garden show. "Tomatoes are like miracle workers. Full of antioxidants and vitamins that strengthen vision, reduce the risk of blood clots, lower the chances of heart disease. On and on. Supposedly, they speed up fat burning capacity by thirty percent."

He frowned and patted his flat abdomen. "Am I looking—"

"Not that you need to lose weight," I said hastily, blushing. Far from it. He had the kind of body women go crazy for. Other women, that is—not me. I just couldn't think of him that way—not with him being my boss. "I just mean tomatoes are so good for us, they might be the best vegetable in the world."

"In that case, maybe I'd better have a couple more."

I dropped three red tomatoes into his open hand. As he curled his palm to keep them from rolling away, the tips of his fingers brushed against my palm and sent a shiver through me. My breath caught.

This conversation had gone on way too long. If he wasn't going to leave, I had to. I could pick vegetables tomorrow. I brushed off my hands and stood. "If you want any more, just help yourself. Sorry to run, but I'm meeting friends."

I made it to the stairwell door before he called, "Kristin. Hey, what was that you said before?"

I turned. "Excuse me?"

Drew was striding toward me. "What did you say about these tomatoes being the best in the world?"

Shit. My heart began to thrum, the sound not unlike the splat of tomatoes hitting the sidewalk after being dropped from a second story window. I had to quit using that phrase; it was going to do me in. My thoughts began to career around the inside of my skull. "Oh, I didn't mean it like they've won an international award or something," I babbled, trying to find a safe path. "Well, they might have won an award, I don't precisely know. I just like them a lot, they're really good but what I meant is that, from the standpoint of healthiness..."

"Have we met before?" His eyes roved over me, taking in every inch of my face, my hair, my clothes, my height, width, depth, and weight. I felt a little like a package about to be shipped by the post office. All he had to ask was whether I was flammable or perishable and I would know I had entered some parallel postal universe.

His demeanor softened. "Sorry. You seem so familiar."

Oh, great. He'd just thrown the ball to me. It was my

decision now. Do I set my steps along the truthful high road or step deeper in the muck of the in-the-gutter low road? Double down on the pretense that we'd never met before, or tell the truth about that morning at continental breakfast?

And by truth, of course, I mean the *slightly revised* truth. Which was that, yes, we'd met at breakfast. And yes, absolutely, I'm a reviewer. And then I'd pull up GetOutaTown.com on my phone and show him the review for Grandad's Donuts—thank God, I put reviews up over lunch—which would be proof positive that I'd done exactly what I'd promised to do that morning after continental breakfast. Even though I'd blown him off.

It was moment of truth time. Okay, okay, moment of *slightly revised* truth time.

I inhaled, ready to spill all, but before I got a word out, Drew asked, "Do you have a sister?"

He waved a hand back and forth. "That sounds bad, let me back up. A few weeks ago, I met a woman who looks like you. I didn't get her name, but—" He shook his head. "It was really early and I'd had a late night, so maybe I'm remembering her wrong and seeing a resemblance where there isn't one. This probably won't make a lot of sense, but do you have a sister who's a restaurant reviewer?"

I didn't answer for so long, I was surprised he didn't think I'd been transformed into a statue of salt like those sinners in the Bible. I opened my mouth to clear up the misunderstanding, to explain that, actually, I was the person he'd met at continental breakfast and I do reviews for GetOutaTown.com. And then it dawned on me that I could blame this all on my sister.

Even though I didn't have a sister.

But he didn't know that.

I could smile and say something like, "Yes, I do have a sister. People are always mistaking us for each other. And, yes, she's a reviewer."

How simple. How stress-free.

How stupid.

Talk about digging a deeper hole.

Before I could thrash the idea any longer, the words I'd intended to say dislodged themselves from my frontal lobe and slipped into my mouth to be sent out into the world. "As a matter of fact," I said slowly, "we have met. A few weeks ago at continental breakfast. I wasn't sure I should bring it up, you being the new president and all."

A grin sprang to his face. "I thought I knew you. Just wasn't sure. You're not exactly the same...and I was pretty tired doing the delivery that morning. I'd already been putting in some long hours behind the scenes here at the catalog."

"Well...and I don't look my best right now. This head cold has had me under the weather." I knew I was supposed to be coming clean, but since this moment of truth was just a continuation of a small white lie, it seemed simpler not to admit I'd been lowering my voice to keep him from recognizing me. I mean, why go there?

"Can I ask, what happened to you that morning?"

Well, no beating around the bush for him. "I lost you at a stoplight. Since I had to get to work, I decided to swing into Grandad's another time and do a review." I swallowed hard. "So that's what I did."

"Really?" He seemed inordinately pleased.

"I'm a woman of my word." I mentally cringed at my word choice. "Grandad's Donuts are just so amazing, how could I not do a review?"

"My brother will be pumped. He owns the place. Thank you." Drew motioned with one hand. "What's the site name? I thought you said it was Get Out of Town but when I tried to pull that up, it didn't work. Figured I got it wrong."

Wait until I told Megan how brilliant she was to change the name. "It's spelled different than it sounds." I spelled it for him, keeping my voice casual, like this was just a typical conversation I had every day.

"No wonder I couldn't find it." He cocked his head. "So you work two jobs?"

"No, no, no. The review thing isn't really a job. I like to try new restaurants. Thought it would be fun to share my experiences, so I started a blog. It's just something I do on the side."

"That's impressive."

I lifted a shoulder in a half shrug, more than a little uncomfortable accepting a compliment for a website that was born of deceit. "So, um, I really need to run," I said, aiming for the doorway.

"I'm sorry. Just tell your friends you had a rooftop rendezvous with the boss. That should shut them up."

Oh, if he only knew. "I'll do that." Anxious to escape before he asked anymore questions, I took the stairs all the way to the first floor. And once I was in my car, I whipped off a text to the girls: *Drew knows who I am.*

I wasn't home twenty minutes before Allie and Bree arrived with a hot pizza and a bottle of red wine. "Moral support has arrived," Allie said, bustling through the door.

Bree followed her in. "Megan sends her regrets. She's still out of town with that deposition."

"You aren't going to believe my day," I said.

"Hold that thought! Wait until the wine has been poured and a glass is in every hand." Bree set the pizza on the coffee table and got plates from the kitchen, while Allie filled three glasses with wine and passed them out.

"Okay, we're ready." Allie dropped into an overstuffed chair. "Tell us everything—"

"And don't leave the details out."

By the time I finished the story about my day—from the meeting with Drew in the morning, to uploading reviews and nearly getting caught by Carly over lunch, to running into Drew on the roof after work—the pizza had been devoured and the wine was nearly gone.

"He bought it all? Everything?" Bree asked. "Hook, line, and sinker?"

"Did you put your shirt in cold water so the tomato stain doesn't set?" Allie interrupted.

I smiled at her motherly concern. "The shirt is soaking. And yes, he bought it all."

Bree leaned forward. "I bet he appreciated that you haven't been running around the company, gossiping about him being a donut deliveryman. He thinks you're trustworthy."

"We can only hope."

"All I have to say is, it's a good thing we made that website," Allie said, sipping her wine. "Just imagine the conversation you and Drew would have had on the roof otherwise."

"Which reminds me, I've got to get the rest of the reviews uploaded." I gulped down the last of my wine and powered up my laptop.

As I uploaded reviews, Allie patted a hand on the armrest of the couch. "This whole thing may have a silver lining. I bet Drew's opinion of you rose the minute he learned you ran your own website. You weren't just a merchandising assistant anymore—suddenly you were an entrepreneur. A business owner. President. CEO."

I looked up from the computer. "A slight stretch. Let's

not forget that, once I finish these uploads, Get Outa Town will have a grand total of eleven reviews. Eleven."

"Allie's right," Bree said. "The fact is, you have a working website. It shows...stick-to-itiveness. Who knows? Maybe this whole nightmare will actually help your career!"

I felt a flicker of unease. I wanted to keep my job. I wanted to get promoted. But I wasn't so sure about building my future on a house of cards called Get Outa Town. The slightest breeze could make the whole thing collapse.

"You know, I just thought of another silver lining. Maybe even a better one." Bree gave me a pointed look. "As long as the cat's out of the bag, you can drop the spinster librarian style."

"Hear, hear." Allie raised her glass.

"Thank God for small favors." I emptied the last of the wine into my glass. "Okay two more reviews to upload and then I've got another project to start."

"How can we possibly do anything else?" Bree picked up the empty bottle. "We're out of wine."

"Nate texted me. He's having a booth at *Taste of Twin Cities* and wants to know how soon we'll have the new donut names."

"Wait, but isn't *Taste* the weekend after next?" Allie set her glass down with a clunk.

I nodded. "Everything seems to be a rush these days.

Chop chop." I pounded the edge of my right hand into the palm of my left.

Bree tipped her chin down and raised her eyes. "Now that Drew knows you're the continental breakfast girl, are you going to tell him you're helping Nate? Or vice versa?"

"For some reason, it feels like a bad idea."

"Maybe because you told Nate your name was Kristine Carlotta," Allie pointed out. "And Drew knows you as Kristin Caruso."

"Oh yeah, there's that. Besides, I'll be done working for Nate before the week is out." I pushed my hair behind my ears, almost missing that stupid bun that kept it confined to the back of my head. "And not a moment too soon. I can't wait for life to go back to normal."

"Kristin, you have too many balls in the air. Just text Nate that new names can't be done that fast," Bree said. "He'll have to do *Taste of Twin Cities* with the current names."

Oh sure, that was the easy answer. Easy for everyone who wasn't the person who expounded about the importance of selling the sizzle not the steak, then proceeded to make a bunch of suggestions and, worst of all, agreed to help the guy make it all happen. "Yeah, that's a great idea—for someone who didn't answer his text by saying Allie and I had been working on new names since leaving the shop yesterday."

"Kristin! Why would you do that?" Allie tilted up her glass to finish the last of her wine.

"Save the world syndrome," Bree said. "I thought you were working on it."

I pressed my lips together and nodded. "I had a relapse. Look, I know I don't owe him anything on such short notice, but you have to admit *Taste of Twin Cities* would be a great opportunity for him to make an impact. How hard can it be, really, to come up with new donut names?" I glanced hopefully between Allie and Bree.

"When?" Bree asked.

I gave a non-committal shrug. "You know, like soon."

"I'm busy every night this week," Allie said.

Bree dropped her head back and laughed. "I don't think the rest of the week is the problem. Just guessing, but I'm thinking we're not going home tonight until we've rechristened every one of Grandad's Donuts."

"What a great idea!" I said, jumping to my feet. "I'll get some paper and pens." I cleaned the pizza mess off the coffee table and went into the kitchen.

"Better bring another bottle of wine, too." Bree slouched into the couch and put up her feet. "To help the creative process."

EIGHT

By the time my alarm blared the next morning, I had already been awake for two hours. I hauled into work, relieved to have something to take my mind off the dreams that had plagued me all night, each one progressively more frightening, and all of them about me pretending to be two people and working like crazy not to get caught.

As I was working my way through the twenty-seven new emails that had arrived since I left work yesterday, and my desk phone started ringing, Melanie swung into my cubicle and skidded to a halt. She gave me an exaggerated once-over. "Is your test over already?"

"My test?" I asked grumpily, ignoring the phone.

"Yeah, the one where you dress like an old lady to see if anyone treats you more seriously."

Oh right. I had my regular clothes on today. And makeup. I picked up the handset. "Kristin Caruso."

"Have you heard back from any of the vendors you called yesterday?" Carly said. "We're on a deadline."

No shit, I wanted to respond, but of course I refrained. "I'm just going through my emails now. I'll let you know when I'm done. I'm sure I'll have everything this afternoon."

"Not soon enough. I just heard from Drew. He rescheduled tomorrow's meeting for three this afternoon. Apparently, he wants a preliminary look to make sure we're on the right path."

"Are you kidding?" I waved a hand at Melanie and whispered, "Drew wants our proposals today."

Her eyes popped wide.

"Do I kid? I'm going to need another cup of coffee," Carly said. "I'm really swamped."

Seriously?

I pushed the speakerphone button so Melanie could hear the exchange right along with me.

"No sugar this time, it's making me jittery. And add more cream...try to match the spots on a Holstein cow."

Melanie put a hand over her mouth to block a laugh.

Unbelievable. In the midst of deadline hell, Carly was getting ridiculous about the color of her coffee. Plus, she obviously hadn't grown up in the Midwest. "Holsteins are black and white," I said peevishly. "Do you mean the spots on a Guernsey cow? Although those can tend to be reddish..."

"Hold on a second."

I could hear her fingernails tapping the keyboard, then a pause. "Oh yes, Guernsey is okay. Or maybe even a Hereford. Make it a large. Half decaf." She cleared her throat. "And, Kristin, for the meeting with Drew, please make sure the conference room has a full pot of fresh coffee and a plate of those donuts. Assorted," she said and hung up.

I looked at Melanie. "Oh, yeah, my test is over. No one takes me seriously no matter what I wear. Especially not Carly."

My desk phone jangled again and we both let out a groan. "CB's out of control today," Melanie said. "I'd better get to my desk before she discovers I'm not there."

"She probably already did, that's why she's calling me again," I said as Melanie dashed away.

I shoved the phone to my ear and snapped, "Do you want me to get through these emails or not?"

My cell phone buzzed and I read the text message on the screen: Printer needs donut names by tomorrow to have new rack cards done before Taste of Twin Cities. Don't want to pressure you, but is it possible?

Ohhhh, I'd always been a firm believer in helping people when they needed help—not just when it was convenient for me. But suddenly, the stress of living that philosophy was like a thousand pound weight on my shoulders.

"Hello?" I said into the phone when Carly didn't reply.

"Excuse me?" came a male voice. "I'm trying to reach Kristin Caruso."

"Oh, yes, no…" I stammered, sitting up straighter. "This is Kristin."

"Oh, good. Kristin, this is Drew Lawson," he said.

Drew? I had just bitched at the company president? My vision seemed to waver for a second, probably from a sudden drop in blood pressure. "Oh, good morning, how are you?"

"Good, good. I have a couple of questions I want to ask you."

Questions? Oh shit. I was doomed. My story would only hold up to only the mildest level of scrutiny. I should have lied last night after all, should have said it was my sister. That we look so much alike and I was trying to protect her because…no one is supposed to know she runs a review website…because she's…married to a famous man who's going to run for public office so she's supposed to keep a low profile. That made sense. Sort of.

I could say all that right now before he was able to ask anything. Just blurt it right out. Drew, I forgot! I got mixed up! I forgot, it's not me—it's my sister! She's the reviewer! Not me! You met her that day, not me. I love working at The Joneses! It's my dream job!

Merchandising assistant.

Fetching coffee for Carly.

"Are you there?" he asked.

"Oh, yes! Questions. Sorry, sometimes my phone has issues." Sigh.

"Have you let maintenance know?"

"It's not that big a deal," I said in a rush. "I just have to hold the cord a certain way and then it's fine. Just fine. Can you hear me now?"

"Yes, great," he said.

I waited for the hammer to come down. For him to say my story didn't add up, that he was disappointed in my lack of integrity—the principle he valued most—and that I should stop into human resources to get the details about my severance package. Except, I was such an *unrecognizable*, my severance package probably involved someone carrying my box of belongings for me as I was escorted out the front door.

"I've been thinking about our conversation last night. About the tomatoes."

What?

"How tomatoes are so healthy."

"Uh, right. Super healthy." I sounded dumb. "Phytonutrients and all that," I quickly added.

"Phyto what?"

I winced, realizing that I probably sounded like one of those pretentious people who throws around million dollar words that no one knows the meaning of. "They're kind of like antioxidants."

Sweat prickled under my arms. What did this guy want from me?

"Anyway, I was just wondering if I could take a few more of your tomatoes."

He was calling because he wanted to score a few tomatoes? "Of course! There's plenty! Help yourself to some good health!" I said in a voice too high and chipper.

"And maybe a couple of carrots and a pepper?"

"Sure, sure!" He could have whatever he wanted, just as long as he didn't bring up continental breakfast. Or my fake sister. Or fire me.

"Making soup?" I quipped, instantly regretting it. Just because he wanted vegetables didn't mean he wanted to be my friend.

A chuckle rumbled out of him, rich and deep. "Something like that. I'll see you at the meeting."

"Right. Okay. See you later." I set the phone back in its cradle, dumbfounded.

Maybe he was hungry. And didn't have change to feed the snack machines. And didn't want to eat any more Grandad's Donuts because, let's face it, a donut a day probably wouldn't keep the doctor away. Not like a tomato would anyway. So maybe he just wanted to have something nutritious. And the only nutritious thing around was my vegetables.

I totally got it. I mean, I was growing the things wasn't I?

Still, it was hard to believe there wasn't something more to his request. I wondered if he was on his way to the roof right now. I pictured him walking over to my garden, reaching out to touch my tomato plants, carefully stroking the branches aside so he could reach into the depths and pluck a tomato from the vine, roll it gently in his fingers, then slip it into his mouth. As he bit into the juicy goodness, his eyes would close and a soft moan would escape from between parted lips—

What was wrong with me? The guy asks for a few vegetables and I create a porno?

I wrested my attention back to Nate's text message and his question about whether we would be able to deliver new donut names by tomorrow. Optimism filled me. Last night, Allie, Bree, and I had nearly finished the whole project; I had only three donuts left to rename.

A deadline of tomorrow wouldn't be a problem—the bigger issue would be fitting in a meeting with Nate. I knew I could mail the finished list to him, but we were proposing some pretty radical name changes, and a quick meeting covering the rationale would be a lot easier than writing something up. I texted him back, and within minutes we agreed to meet at the crack of dawn—six-thirty in the morning. If Allie couldn't make it, I'd just go alone.

The ringing of my desk phone interrupted my thoughts; with a sigh, I picked up yet another call from Carly.

"Sorry...but my coffee?" she asked when I picked up.

Sorry? There wasn't a speck of apology in her voice. "I'll get that right now."

"Don't forget, Guernsey cow brown."

I hung up the phone, dropped my head to my desk, and sighed out a long, sad, "Moooo."

"Our goal is to meet our go-to market at the place where they know that their worth is embraced." Carly strolled across the front of the conference room, smiling at Drew like she was a C-suite executive giving a motivational speech to an audience of thousands—instead of in a cramped conference room with Melanie, James, Drew, three guys from the marketing department, and me.

"Toward that end, we've been thinking outside the box, reaching out to vendors for win-win suggestions that will enable The Joneses to offer a robust product line that demonstrates authenticity for purchasers while simultaneously maximizing ROI."

I sneaked a glance at the marketing guys. They looked enthralled. Melanie on the other hand, had two fingers pressed to her chin.

"Creative destruction," one of the marketing guys said.

"Exactly." Carly nodded triumphantly.

Whatever.

"My team has been burning the candle at both ends," Carly blathered. "And I'm pleased to present a broad range of new product ideas across a wide spectrum of verticals that, I think you will agree, will not just grow mind share, but will bring synergy to the catalog."

"Synergy. And mind-share," Drew said, nodding. "Sounds good. Let's see what you've got."

Carly pressed a few keys, and the presentation deck on her laptop was instantly projected on the electronic smart screen on the wall. "Of course, this is only the kicking off point, but I think it aligns with your vision for the catalog. I'm confident these products will help move the graph up and to the right."

A photo filled the screen—the two-man, whale-shaped submarine that I'd found yesterday—and Carly dove into a detailed description. Facts and figures, length and width, blahdy, blah, blah. After a minute of boring minutiae that I already knew, my brain began to glaze over. I came back into the discussion just as one of the marketing guys was saying, "...could be visionary. Featured on the catalog's cover, it could be symbolic of *The Joneses* paradigm shift."

I wondered if Drew knew about the upcoming paradigm shift at Grandad's Donuts, that Nate was about to shake up his company's image in a big way—as soon as we created names for the last three donuts, anyway.

Carly brought up a picture of a diamond-studded chess set. "Each chess piece is white gold and inset with white or black diamonds. Ten thousand in all." She began to run through the details. "This handmade set retails for five hundred thousand dollars..."

One of the donuts that stumped us last night was a type of apple fritter. Nate's apple fritters were so amazing —with apples and blueberries inside, and topped with cream cheese frosting—we wanted an amazing new name. Something descriptive and clever like... *The Big Apple.*

Ugh, stupid.

I tuned back into Carly's presentation to make sure I wasn't missing anything. She was droning on, saying something about, "...would position us as an agent of change, a mover and shaker..." and I nodded as though I was hanging on every word, but my brain was firmly wrapped around apple blueberry fritters.

Apple dapple. Apple dappling. Dabbling in apples. Blueberry Apple. BlueApple. Blapple. Blapple? Maybe it was time to tack in a different direction.

The picture on the screen switched to one of a large, lavish camp tent outfitted with a crystal chandelier and expensive furnishings. "I admit that when I first saw this tent—at seventy-five thousand dollars—it took my breath away," Carly said. "But for people who want to experience the great outdoors without any of the nasty discomforts, this is the perfect tent for glamour camping, that new trend known as *glamping.* I believe this would have *ultimate ap-peal* to our target market."

Ultimate appeal. How did she know what appealed to rich people? Maybe rich people wanted to rough-it once in a while. Maybe rich people would look at a diamond chess set and think to themselves: *Just one more thing to dust.*

Then again, maybe not, since they probably don't do their own dusting.

Ul-ti-mate. App-eal, my mind repeated. *Ultimate Apple*

Peel. Although, peel wasn't a very *appealing* word. Excuse the pun. I let out a snort, and everyone in the room turned to me.

"Sorry. Tried to hold in a sneeze. Just getting over a cold." I gave my nose a rub and motioned for Carly to continue.

Okay, so apple blueberry fritters. Apples are red and blueberries are, well, blue. How about an all-American themed name along the lines of Yankee Doodle? Something like *Apple Dandy.* Or maybe... *Apple Doodle Dandy.*

Ooh, that had potential. I wrote *Apple Doodle Dandy* in small letters on my notepad so I wouldn't forget it.

The marketing men were deep in discussion, the latest business jargon peppering their sentences. "...feeds into our core competencies..." "...an idea that is definitely scalable..." "...the one percent price point..."

There was so much jargon bouncing around the room, I was beginning to wonder if the people using it even knew what they were saying. Or did it just make them feel important to use phrases that other people didn't understand? Still, it probably wouldn't hurt for me to get up to speed on business-speak so I could jaw with the big guys in case opportunities for advancement arose. I scribbled *core competencies* and *scalable* on my sheet, along with something one of them said earlier, *mind-share.* I could make a reasonable guess at what these meant, but it wouldn't hurt to be sure.

By that point, Carly was blabbing something about "... next gen plug and play..." and "...the latest cutting edge technology..." James threw me a look that screamed sheer boredom, and I answered with an almost imperceptible shrug of the shoulders. Every department meeting was always The Carly Show, and even a new president wasn't going to change that.

Carly brought up a picture of the full wall aquarium— dumbest product ever—while I brought up a mental picture of Nate's chocolate custard-filled donut. Striped across the top with three different types of chocolate frosting—dark, white, and milk—then topped with two fresh cherries. Drew called it *Triple Chocolate*, but all I wanted to call it was decadent.

Carly kept talking, the marketing guys kept asking questions, and donut name options filled my thoughts: *Decadent Delight. Indulge your Fantasies. Ménage á Chocolat.*

I tried to remember my high school French, but I got a C plus in the class, and I only got the plus because I cheated in the language lab. But everyone knows that *Ménage á trois* means love triangle. So, *Ménage á Chocolat* had to mean a love triangle of chocolate. What a perfect donut name!

I started to write it down, then stopped. Wait. *Trois* was French for *three*, so without *trois* in the name, *Ménage á Chocolat* meant...shit, what did it mean? What did *ménage* actually translate to? It would have to be *Chocolat á Trois,* wouldn't it? Or *Ménage á Trois Chocolat*. I tapped my pen lightly on my notepad, thinking.

"...and I have to say it was inspired by Kristin."

Did I just hear my name? I blinked, gradually becoming aware that everyone was looking at me. What was going on? I watched as Drew lifted a paper bag from the floor next to his chair and set three cherry tomatoes, a carrot, and a green pepper on the table. My garden vegetables.

Carly leveled a steely-eyed gaze on me. Melanie and James were grinning like they were ready to pop. *What was going on?*

"Organic, fresh vegetables. About the healthiest thing you can eat," Drew said.

"What is it the experts recommend? Five fruits or vegetables a day," Carly gushed.

What were they all talking about? Mailing vegetables to rich people? First of all, fresh vegetables weren't that hard to come by, and they weren't all that expensive either —not compared to diamond-studded chess sets anyway. It made no sense for The Joneses to sell fresh vegetables through the catalog.

"It's a healthy indulgence. Great idea, Drew. Really unique," one of the marketing guys said as the others bobbed their heads in agreement.

What a bunch of suck-ups. This wasn't a great idea. The emperor was naked and no one had the guts to say it. I know I vowed to stop trying to save the world, but this idea was so ridiculous, I owed it to Drew to be the voice of reason in the room.

I held up a hand and assumed a caring, yet pragmatic demeanor. "There are already quite a few online sites where people can order fresh vegetables. And the number of organic grocery stores just keeps growing. Not to mention farmer's markets where people can buy veggies fresh from the farm." I kept my tone light to lessen the negative impact of my words.

"Yes, but you have to admit this is a bit more indulgent," Drew said.

"Mailing vegetables?"

Melanie kicked me under the table.

Drew smiled. "Mailing a greenhouse."

My blood stopped flowing. A greenhouse? A glass walled building where plants grow? We weren't talking about mailing vegetables? He wanted to put a greenhouse in the catalog? I looked at Melanie; her slow, surreptitious nod confirmed my guess.

"Right...the greenhouse...that would be put up..." I watched Melanie for any sign I was going in the wrong direction. "...on their property. So they can pick their own fresh vegetables every day."

Melanie lowered her chin and rubbed her brow to indicate approval.

Come on. A greenhouse. Ordered from a catalog. Delivered door-to-door. Probably set up by experts. Stocked with plants. I was having a little problem visualizing the ultra-wealthy working in a greenhouse, even one they ordered themselves. Think about it—the fertilizing, the cultivating, the watering, the weeding, the bug-killing, the thinning, the picking.

"Maybe a gardener should be included to do the work," I said. "The ultimate luxury."

Drew picked up a tomato, rolled it in the fingers of one hand, then slipped it into his mouth. His eyes met mine and my breath snagged and I quickly scribbled some nonsensical shit on my notepad so I seemed like I was all business, all the time.

"I'm not sure we want to get into the business of providing employees," he said. "Too many complications. But I'd like us to do some quick research. See if offering a greenhouse is even feasible. What I'm picturing are big, solid greenhouses—not those do-it-yourself thousand dollar shed things."

Everyone nodded, no one more than Carly. "I'll jump on it as soon as we wrap here," she said. Which meant that Melanie, James, or I—maybe all three of us—would soon be on the job finding greenhouses that would make Carly a star.

Drew put the carrot and pepper back in the paper bag. "Appreciate that, Carly, but Kristin and I were talking yesterday, and I discovered she's quite the gardener. So let's put her in charge of chasing this down." He turned to the marketing guys. "Gentlemen, let's regroup in my office in half an hour."

"And Kristin," he said, picking up the two remaining cherry tomatoes. "Can you have something tomorrow afternoon, maybe around this same time?"

"I'll check my schedule," Carly said as she pulled up the calendar on her phone.

Drew looked at her for a long moment. "No need for you to be there, Carly. I'm sure you have more important things to do. Kristin can show me what she finds." The smile he gave me was so warm, I thought I might melt. "Let's say, my office at two-thirty."

"Sounds great," I said in a strangled voice, my face flushing red.

Drew dropped one of the tomatoes in the bag, then popped the other into his mouth and bit down. For a moment, I stared, mesmerized, then I jerked my attention to the pad of paper in front of me, determined to crush my overactive imagination by concentrating on my job. I scrawled *research greenhouse with vegetables* across the top of the page, right above *Apple Doodle Dandy*. Words I'd written earlier seemed to pop out at me: *Decadent. Indulge. Fantasies. Ménage á Trois.* My body seemed to be humming.

I circled *research greenhouse with vegetables* three times to center my thoughts.

It didn't help.

NINE

Soft, early morning light illuminated Grandad's Donuts, and the luscious scent of fresh donuts wafted through the room. Nate, Allie, and I were at a table near the front window, each with a mug of hot coffee, a platter of donuts in front of us.

"When I die, I want the scent of fresh donuts at my funeral," Allie said. "Not candles or incense. Grandad's Donuts."

"That's a compliment...right?" Nate asked.

I broke off a piece of one of the donuts and put it in my mouth. The rich, spicy flavor of maple frosted gingerbread woke up every one of my taste buds. I was more convinced than ever that the names we'd coined would help Grandad's Donuts break out of the crowd.

I patted the red folder I had set on the table when we arrived. "Before we show you the new names, let me set the stage. Did you know that most people make decisions based on emotion, then justify them with fact?"

"I would have thought it's the other way around."

"Nope. So our goal was to make each donut name trigger an emotional response in the customer."

"Joy, love, connectedness, pride, any good memories really," Allie added.

I put another piece of gingerbread donut in my mouth and licked the frosting off my index finger. "Like this delicious donut that I can't stop eating even in a meeting. You call it a Gingerbread Donut. But what if you lift a line from the folktale, The Gingerbread Man, and call the donut, *Can't Catch Me*?"

"I've run away from a little old woman, I've run away from a little old man," Allie recited. "You can't catch me, I'm the gingerbread man."

"The description, *Can't Catch Me, gingerbread donut*, will trigger childhood memories of being read *The Gingerbread Man*. Your donut will be instantly associated with warm memories of family and love and safety and childhood. And who wouldn't want to remember that?"

Nate sat back in his chair, his whole face alight. "Wow. When I opened this business I just figured, make a good donut and customers would come. I didn't put much thought into people's expectations."

"There's so much competition for people's money these days," I said, thinking of The Joneses audience. "To get attention, you have to offer more than just a great product.

In a sense, you need to offer *an experience*. So, every donut tells a story. Every story triggers emotions."

"And every emotion triggers sales," Allie said triumphantly.

The amazement on Nate's face told me he was completely on board.

"So without further ado—" I flipped open the folder. "Let's see what you think about the names we've come up with."

"I like them all. Sight unseen."

A laugh burbled out of me. Why was it that this guy thought I was brilliant, while over at The Joneses no one ever saw me as anything more than an assistant?

I handed him and Allie each a sheet printed with the current Grandad's Donut list on the left, and the new names on the right. "Here's what we've come up with. A couple of donuts have two names listed because we couldn't decide which was best. You get to pick."

As Nate perused the list, his smile grew. "I don't know what to say. These are fantastic. Before, I was selling donuts. Now each one is a story."

Allie and I exchanged a happy look. "Good answer," she said.

"I don't know how to thank you."

"Donuts!" we said in unison.

"I can't wait to see the response at *Taste of Twin Cities*," Drew said. "If you have any ideas for improving our booth, I'm open to suggestions. This is my first year so the plan was pretty simple—put up a tent and make sure we have donuts to sell." He gave the page of donut names a shake. "But after this, maybe there's something more I should be doing."

"We can give it some thought," Allie said, beaming.

Obviously, flattery made her forget that I wanted to end our association with Nate—not keep it going. I tucked my hair behind my ears and sent her a telepathic warning.

"Actually, it's up to Kris—tine," she added hastily as if she'd gotten the message. "She's the creative brains. I'm just...support. And, uhh, we're pretty busy these days."

I restrained myself from rolling my eyes.

Nate rubbed his jaw. "I understand if you don't have time. I'm asking a lot on short notice. As you've probably been able to tell..." Discouragement seeped into his voice. "I can use all the help I can get."

He needed help. Arghhhhh. "I'll give it some thought," I said.

Early that afternoon, as the clock ticked closer to my meeting with Drew, I frantically organized the information I'd gathered about greenhouses, cross-referencing by manufacturer, price, size, and design. I stopped in the restroom to touch up my makeup to make sure I looked both professional and attractive. I brushed my teeth with the travel toothbrush I kept in my desk for just such moments. Then I went back to my desk and tried to ignore the nerves making my hands tremble, tried not to think about the fact that I was about to have a one-on-one with Drew Lawson.

Hopefully he'd like what I'd found. Hopefully I would be able to speak coherently. Hopefully he wouldn't have his sleeves cuffed up again. *Hopefully he wouldn't be eating any cherry tomatoes.*

Laptop in hand, I headed upstairs to Drew's office.

"Go on in," his assistant said. "He got caught in another meeting, but said to tell you he won't be more than five minutes."

I'd never been in the president's office before. I set my laptop on the round table in the corner, then pivoted to take in the room. It was like something out of Wealthy Decorating magazine—if there were such a publication. Exactly as I would have pictured for the president of The Joneses. A dark cherrywood desk with an inlaid leather top, gilded framed paintings, two navy patterned upholstered wingback chairs across from the desk, a thick oriental rug over the short nap carpeting. The atmosphere was quiet, still, formal. Except the bookshelf along the wall; the shelves were empty save for a few randomly scattered books and a trophy.

I stepped over to take a closer look at the trophy. On the front was a brass plaque engraved with *First Place Team, Ride Across Florida.*

"From my wilder, younger days."

I spun to see Drew standing in the doorway. "Oh, I'm just—" Just what? Nosing around in his office? I gestured toward the trophy. "Just curious. It's the only thing on the shelf."

"Those shelves were packed with thirty years of things my dad collected, including plenty of items that were strategically purchased to reinforce The Joneses image—reproduction sculptures, oriental vases, rows of classic books he never read. I sent everything home with him and told him to crack some of the bindings."

I stifled a laugh. "The whole office feels very..."

"Stuffy?"

My laughter escaped. I couldn't believe I was hearing this out of the man who was doubling down on positioning The Joneses as a catalog for only the super, ultra, mega rich. "I was going to say *expensive*."

"All a matter of perspective." He picked up the trophy. "This is from a bike race across Florida—almost two hundred miles. We were in college and someone found out about this ride. You know how these things go. You're drinking beer at a party and someone gets an idea. The next thing you know, four of you have formed a team and signed up online. Money's paid, you're committed."

"I may have made some decisions while drinking that didn't seem so smart the next day, but I've never signed up for a two hundred mile bike ride." I shook my head. "So you signed up drunk and then went out and won it?"

His mouth curved in a proud, slightly abashed grin.

"The team category. All team members had to cross the finish line at the same time."

"But you *won*. That's kind of amazing."

"We were young, healthy, in good shape, and dumb enough to believe we could do it."

As if he was now old and in bad shape. I watched him, almost mesmerized as he set the trophy back on the shelf.

"Someone asked me once, what describes you best—*do you like to win or hate to lose?* Turns out, I hate to lose." He began to unbutton his shirt cuffs. "You want to show me what you've got?" he asked.

Electricity jolted through me, squeezing the air out of my lungs. "What I've got?"

He tipped his chin toward my laptop as he gave each cuff a double roll. "I can't wait to see what you've found out about greenhouses."

God, I was a moron. I stumbled back to the table and plopped awkwardly into a one of the chairs, beginning to talk the moment I landed. "At first I wasn't sure this was a good idea," I said, opening my computer. "But then I discovered greenhouses come in an amazing variety of sizes, shapes and styles." My words were coming too fast, but I couldn't stop myself.

Drew had pulled a chair right next to mine so we could both see the computer screen at the same time; I could hardly breathe for the nearness of him. "My favorites are the conservatories. The beauty and elegance of them is, well, beyond the pale." *Beyond the pale? Where did that come from? What did that mean? Was I using it correctly?* What was wrong with me? "I think a conservatory, much more than a greenhouse, would appeal to people with unlimited disposable income." I paused to organize my thoughts.

"Any pictures?" he prompted.

"Oh, yes, of course." I began to click through a series of visuals. "At the big box home improvement stores, greenhouses range from five hundred to fifteen thousand dollars. But for obvious reasons, I think The Joneses customers would prefer something more like this." I brought up a picture of an elaborate greenhouse that looked like it belonged on a castle. "Prince Charming would be right at home," I quipped.

"And Cinderella, too, once he finally found her," Drew teased, his mouth twitching. My heart stammered and I wrenched my eyes back to the computer screen.

"Not only does this one include a greenhouse, but it also has a conservatory with living space. Imagine what it would be like to have a room like this." I showed him a series of fabulous buildings with glass roofs and walls. "The line between indoors and outdoors is totally blurred. Imagine relaxing on one of these comfy, overstuffed sofas or chairs, yet feeling like you're part of nature."

Drew nodded. "The best of all worlds. Fresh, organic vegetables every day. And an amazing space to connect with the outdoors."

"Exactly. I love the octagonal conservatory," I enthused, spreading my arms wide. "This next one feels like it belongs in an English garden. See how the window muntins artistically break up the expanse of glass against the backdrop of nature? These rooms transcend being an indoor garden and become works of art." Okay, I stole that last line from one of the websites, but no need to tell Drew.

"So, it's safe to assume you would buy a conservatory greenhouse?"

I almost said, *Good one!* and asked whether he'd had a chance to review employee salaries yet—specifically merchandising assistant—but decided he probably wasn't making a joke. "I—ah—if I had that kind of money to burn? Well..." I glanced at the ceiling so I didn't have to look directly at him. "I mean, it would be awesome...must be incredible when it's raining, and your ceiling and walls are made of glass. I'm not that big on washing windows, although if I could afford a conservatory, I could probably afford to hire a window washer." I finally met his gaze because there was only so long I could avoid it. "So to answer your question—yes, I would buy one..."

Drew's brows were drawn together. "But? I heard a *but* at the end of that sentence."

"There's not a *but*."

"You can't take it back now. What's the *but* about?"

This was why I always lost at poker when we played for pennies with Grandma. "The thing is, for me—and I'm only talking about me—greenhouse vegetables never taste as good as vegetables grown outside. Maybe it's the rain.

Or the dirt. Or the wind blowing through the leaves as they grow. Who knows?"

I lifted both hands palm up. "A conservatory would be amazing, and a greenhouse would mean I could have fresh vegetables year round, so I totally see the benefits." I pursed my lips, choosing my words. "But for me, I'd have to have an outdoor garden, too. Obviously, you've never done it so you don't know. But if you ever do, you'll understand why, someday, I'm going to have a garden that's bigger than just some pots on a roof."

Drew had half a smile on his face.

I wanted to smack myself in the head. Too much detail. Too much blabbering detail. My cheeks heated, and I clicked through some more photos. "Here are some other greenhouse and conservatory options," I said, all business again. "As you can see, there's a variety of options and princes. I mean, prices." I should never have brought up Prince Charming.

"How about plants? Can we offer a greenhouse ready to go?"

I opened another window on the computer. "There are a few options. Some seed companies even sell starter plants. The one I like best, though, is a local grower—Friendly Frank's Farm Fresh Foods. He has a big stand at the farmer's market every week, and already has an online plants-in-the-mail business. Ships nationwide."

"Friendly Frank's, huh?" Drew gave me an appreciatory nod. "I'd like to talk to him."

I brought up Frank's website. "His phone number is in the presentation. I'll forward you the whole thing when we're done."

"I'd like to meet him." Drew sat back in his chair. "Is he at the farmer's market every week?"

"He's been there whenever I am, and that's pretty often."

Drew rubbed a hand over his jaw. "Why don't we go together this weekend? You can introduce us, and I can get a feel for his business and how we can work together."

The room seemed to buzz. How had we just segued from a presentation on greenhouses to me taking Drew to the farmer's market on Saturday? "The farmer's market gets really busy. He might not be able to talk for long."

"That's all right. I like seeing people in their element. Gives me a better sense of what they're really like. What time do you usually go?"

Under other circumstances, I might be ecstatic to spend time with a guy like Drew. But between him being the new company president, the lies I'd told at continental breakfast, the fact that I was working for his brother under a fake name, well, I had way too many irons in a fire that was probably hot enough to melt lead. So in my mind, the less time we spent together, the better. I opened my mouth to say I wasn't going to the farmer's market this weekend because I had other plans. No need for him to know that my only plans involved walking dogs for the animal shelter. Plans were plans.

And then a really critical piece of information jammed its way to the front of my brain.

Drew was in the middle of a reorganization. Rumor had it he was compiling a termination list, the names of everyone who would lose their jobs in the weeks ahead. Getting on his good side might be a very beneficial thing. And going to the farmer's market with him on Saturday just might put me there. I couldn't believe I was going to agree to this. "It opens at seven, but I usually arrive about nine."

"Great. I'll meet you there."

TEN

"HE WANTS TO GO TO THE FARMER'S MARKET?" JAMES pushed some change into the snack machine and retrieved a bag of potato chips from the slot.

"Just you and Drew?" Melanie chimed in. "What do you think this means?"

I gave her a look like she'd lost her mind. "It doesn't mean anything."

"Drew wants to spend his Saturday at the farmer's market with you, and you think there's no hidden meaning? This isn't James we're talking about—"

"What's wrong with me?" he asked, munching on a potato chip.

"You eat so much crap, they probably wouldn't even let you in the farmer's market." Melanie shook her head. "You should try those vitamin smoothies I sell. No fat, no sugar, and they're delicious. Right, Kristin?"

James already knew I thought they were awful. "Right," I said. "You should get some, James."

"I'll think about it," he said, around a mouthful of chips.

Melanie sighed. "Anyway, my point is, we're talking about the company president, the hottie at the helm," Melanie said. "What if this is actually a date?"

Suddenly I could picture her calling Nicole in human resources, the head of *Joneses Gossip Central.* Within half an hour, word would be all over the company that I was going out with the president. God only knew how much the story would be embellished as it passed from person to person. God only knew how Drew would react if he thought I was spreading rumors that I was dating the boss. Can you say: *new name added to the termination list?*

"I don't have a date with Drew," I said with conviction.

"Someone has a date with Drew?" Carly came into the vending machine alcove and began to peruse the snack options.

No one answered.

"Is there something going on with Drew I should know about?" she asked in her poison voice.

"No," Melanie said at the same moment, I said "Drew wants to go to the farmer's market with me."

James chewed loudly on a potato chip, and Carly scowled at him. "That's so unhealthy, James. Now, what is this date with Drew?"

"It's not a date," I said, emphasizing each word. "He

wants to meet a farmer about sourcing plants for the greenhouse idea. At the farmer's market on Saturday morning. I happen to know the guy. It's not a date, it's business."

"Obviously," Carly sniped.

"Excuse me?" I asked, biting my tongue to keep myself from saying something much worse.

"With all due respect, Kristin, you're a merchandising assistant," she said.

"And a damn good one," I shot back.

"Overqualified," Melanie added loyally.

Carly got a red delicious apple from the vending machine and held it up in front of James. He shoved some more potato chips in his mouth.

I couldn't cope with this. Not the stress of Carly knowing, not the pressure of having two full days to think about Saturday before it actually happened. I wanted to slap myself in the head for letting it slip. I opened my mouth to jump back into the fray, but James clamped a hand over my forearm and let out a jovial chuckle.

"Maybe Kristin will be able to get some inside information that'll let us quit worrying about our jobs," he said. "Carly, this Saturday business junket might end up helping us."

After a long pause, she dipped her chin in acknowledgement. "Keep in mind that while you and Drew are enjoying the farmer's market on Saturday, the rest of us will be here in the office working to meet our deadlines."

Then she launched into a description of the *inside information* she'd recently learned—that human resources wanted all department heads to review and revise job descriptions for each person in their department. It didn't take a genius to know that *presentations of new product ideas to the president* would soon be a responsibility listed in her job description only, while *schlepping coffee and donuts* would soon be a bullet point only in mine.

Thursday and Friday passed uneventfully at work—mostly because Drew was out of town and the rest of us had so much to get done to meet the aggressive timetable that had been established for the catalog overhaul. Even Allie, Megan, and Bree took the news of my farmer's market trip with Drew in stride—at least I thought they did, until we met for Friday night happy hour at MinneTiki, a new tropical-themed bar with a Polynesian vibe and a nod to Minneapolis in its name. Once we had exotic drinks and appetizers in front of us, suddenly they had plenty to say.

I pulled the paper umbrella out of my Mai Tai and waved it at them like a sword. "How many times over how many days do I have to say this? It's not a date. It's research gathering. Fact-finding. A business trip."

"Ohhh, research gathering." Megan gave a knowing nod.

"Fact-finding," Allie added.

"I've got a big picture of the whole thing," Bree said in a serious voice. "But, what kind of facts will you be finding? The facts of life?" She batted her lashes at me as she took a swallow of daiquiri.

Allie chortled. "There's something happening here…"

I shut my eyes for a moment and let out a long-suffering sigh. The sound of waves crashing on the shore rolled out of a speaker to my right, while beach party music was playing from the speakers above the bar. It made me long to return to the oceanfront vacation we'd been on just a few weeks ago. "This place almost feels like we're back in the Outer Banks," I said.

"Don't try to change the subject." Allie stopped with a chicken wing halfway to her mouth, barbeque sauce dripping from her fingertips. "I just can't believe how this turned out. You meet the new company president at continental breakfast a few weeks ago and now you're going on a date."

"Allie! We're checking out vegetables and meeting a grower. It's just part of my job. This isn't a date. It's not a Continental Breakfast Club success story."

"That's right," Megan said. "But it does beg the question, what happens if he wants to check out *your* vegetables?"

This? Out of Megan?

"And further, will you be helping him—or a specific part of him—become a grower?" Bree asked.

Oh my God. "Say it with me," I said through gritted teeth. "Research gathering."

"Research gathering," all three dutifully recited, grinning.

"*Business Trip.*" I swiped a celery stick in some French dressing and crunched out a bite.

"*Business. Trip,*" they repeated like robots.

Bree beamed. "It may be a business trip now, but who knows—"

"Stop it! I'm not even interested in this guy. Okay, fine, I could be, but you know *I can't be.*" I slapped a hand on the table. "Quit messing around. This is serious."

My phone vibrated. I was tempted to ignore it because I was getting alerts left and right lately—notifications of texts, emails, tweets, breaking news from NewYorkTimes.com, friend requests on Facebook, you name it. Though I kept planning to deactivate all the alerts so my phone would quit buzzing, at that moment I was happy for anything to derail the direction of our conversation.

I glanced at the screen, then picked up my phone and held it up for the girls. "The strangest thing is happening," I said. "At first I thought it was a mistake, but now I'm not so sure. People are starting to follow *Get Outa Town.* Four days ago, I had four followers—us. Now I have twenty-five."

"Organic growth." Megan narrowed her eyes as though considering what it might mean for us.

"Maybe you've gone viral!" Allie exclaimed. "This is what every blogger dreams of—getting noticed!"

"Twenty-five new followers doesn't sound all that viral. Two hundred and fifty maybe, but not twenty-five," Bree pointed out.

Megan stirred her drink with the straw, not responding for several long seconds. "I don't know if anything has gone viral, but I just thought of something. What's to stop Drew from checking out Get Outa Town in a month?"

I didn't understand her point. "Why would that matter?"

"The site has eleven reviews. If he looks at Get Outa Town a month from now and there's nothing new, he might think you're too busy to put anything up. Or, he could wonder what's going on and start asking questions." She shook her head. "Why even leave the door cracked open to that possibility? You know me—plan for the best, prepare for the worst."

"Whatever can go wrong, will." I dropped my chin into my hand. "My life motto these days. So we need to keep putting reviews up."

"At least for a while. Let a few months pass and, eventually, we can take the site down. If Drew ever asks— and I doubt he will—you say it was fun while it lasted, but it took too much time. Or you lost interest. Whatever feels most logical to you."

Allie put a hand on my arm. "Jax and I are going to dinner tomorrow night. Wherever we end up, I'll write a review about it," she volunteered. "Bree, you and Adam can do the same thing."

"I'll review this place," I said, admiring the bamboo hut decor. "It's new. It's unique. And, between the four of us, we've already tried four different drinks—Mai Tai, Daiquiri, Scorpion, and—" I nudged Megan. "What are you having again?"

"Ancient Mariner...and it's delicious." She took a slurp on her straw to emphasize the point.

Allie picked up the drink menu and waved for our server, a blond surfer kind of guy in an island floral shirt. "We can't review this place without sharing a Flaming Volcano. It's their specialty."

The sky was clear, the sun bright when I arrived at the farmer's market the next morning, determined to make quick work of introducing Drew to Friendly Frank. Once the two of them were deep in conversation, I planned to make an excuse and take off. My coworkers may have believed this was the perfect opportunity for me to get the inside scoop about what was going on with the company, but for me it was shaping up to be just another opportunity for more stress.

Especially after sharing a Flaming Volcano with the girls the night before.

Rum, brandy, pineapple juice, orange juice, you name it—just the thought of what was in that cocktail was enough to make me queasy that morning. Luckily, I didn't imbibe nearly as much as the others had. As soon as the server brought out the huge volcano-shaped drink bowl with its flaming center and four straws protruding out in different directions, I realized that a hot lava hangover might not be the best thing to have when I joined the company president on a research gathering expedition.

I spotted Drew across the parking lot and waved. He held up a cup of coffee, and my mouth watered at the sight. Caffeine was first on the agenda. As soon as I drew near, he said, "They sell coffee and sweet rolls. Belgium waffles. Pancakes. It's not just vegetables."

"You thought the farmer's market only had vegetables?"

"Yeah. Maybe because it's called a *farmer's* market," he said in mock defensive.

I laughed. "That's just the beginning. There's also cheese, honey, pies, jewelry, so many different stands." I bought a large coffee, added a hefty dose of cream, and took a big gulp. Ahhh, just what I needed to wake up.

"Grandad's Donuts should have a stand here. I wonder if Nate has ever looked into it," Drew mused.

"He'd probably sell a lot of donuts. Saturday at the farmer's market always feels a little like being on vacation."

His brow furrowed. "Not sure I get the connection."

"You know how when you're on vacation, you splurge on café coffee instead of making it in your room? And instead of eating a bowl of soggy cereal, you treat yourself to a donut—or if they taste as good as Grandad's, you have two—just because you're on vacation."

He just looked at me.

"That's not your vacation experience?" I asked.

"I buy coffee every day. And if I want a donut..."

"You just have one."

"Right."

So much for simple pleasures. Maybe his definition of vacation was five-star restaurants recommended by concierges at five-diamond hotels. And helicopter tours instead of hikes. "Well, today, just pretend you're on vacation with the regular folk."

He tipped the paper cup to his mouth. "This is the best coffee I've ever had."

"Good start." I patted his arm.

"Okay, so where are we going first?"

First? "Friendly Frank's stand is over that way." I pointed to the far end of the sprawling farmer's market.

Drew turned the opposite direction. "I'm sure he's not going anywhere. Do you think we could walk around a while so I can see more of this?"

So much for introducing him to Frank and escaping.

Sipping our coffee, we stopped near a three piece band

playing folk music. "It's almost like a street festival," Drew said.

I nodded. "Hence, the vacation vibe I mentioned earlier."

"I feel it." He gave a quick smile. "I mean it. Really."

For some reason, his words lifted my heart.

We walked along the rows of booths, trying samples of vegetables—a slice of carrot, a pea pod, a radish. "Everything is fresh picked," I said. "That's why it all tastes so good. It hasn't been loaded on a truck and shipped three states away."

Drew headed across the aisle to taste some salsa. "You have to try this." He scooped a tortilla chip into a bowl of salsa and held it out to me, sauce dripping from its edges.

I started to reach for it, but as the salsa trickled down his hand I shook my head and opened my mouth instead. He fed me the chip and swiped a drop off my chin with his thumb.

"That's amazing. What's the flavor?" I asked around the mouthful of chip.

"Peach."

"I'll take a jar of that," I said to the woman behind the counter. "Peach salsa."

"Two." Drew gave her a twenty dollar bill, picked up two jars, and handed me one. "On me."

On him? I pictured peach salsa on Drew. "Oh, there's the goat milk soap," I said, hoping to distract my suddenly overheated body. "I love that stuff." I charged over to the soap booth while Drew got his change from the salsa lady.

"What's so great about this soap?" He asked, so close to me his breath tickled my neck and my knees almost gave out.

"It's, ah, good for your skin. Non-drying," I read aloud off the sign, then looked to the middle-aged woman behind the counter for help.

"It's very moisturizing because of the cream in goat's milk," the woman said. "You'll love how it makes your skin feel—soft, smooth, satiny. You'll love how it makes *her* skin feel." She handed an information card to Drew, while I tried to banish the mental image of Drew running his hands over my...satiny skin.

"Very moisturizing," I said with a gulp.

"Maintaining healthy skin keeps you youthful." She held a bar out to Drew. "And it's high in Vitamin A, which repairs damaged skin tissue and fine lines."

Why was she looking at me like that? I couldn't possibly have crow's feet already, could I? I touched the outside corner of my eye to see if I could feel the beginning of lines.

"Okay, you've sold me." Drew said. "I'll take one."

"I'll take two," I chimed in.

As we walked away, Drew lifted the bar of soap to his nose. "Smells good, too. Can you believe her spiel? Completely designed to make women fixate on aging."

My cheeks warmed. "Really? I didn't notice."

"But if it does what she says, well who am I to criticize." He touched my arm. "But you, Kristin Caruso, are the last person who needs goat's milk soap for wrinkles."

What about for satiny, soft skin? my mind purred as my thoughts spiraled in erotic directions. I mentally tied a leash around my brain and yanked backward, commanding, *Heel!* This was the company president. And the only reason I was here with him today was to try to keep my job.

We ate chocolate-dipped strawberries as we strolled the crowded market, laughing together as strawberry juice dribbled over our lips and we dabbed our chins dry with the kind of small white napkin you get at the ice cream parlor. We tasted fresh honey and tested cornbread with orange honey butter and tried the crepes.

"I take it you never go home hungry from the farmer's market," Drew said as we stopped at a booth featuring Wisconsin cheese.

I reached for the toothpick stuck through the top of a bite-size piece of Gouda. "You know how they say there's no such thing as a free lunch? That doesn't apply to here."

"Try the bleu cheese." Drew said.

I popped a piece into my mouth.

"Ummm, this Asiago is absolutely amazing," a woman's voice floated over the crowd.

I froze. There was no way, there was just no way—

"Did you try the cheddar? I'm dreaming of deep-fried cheese curds," a male voice replied.

My heart stopped beating. I twisted round just as Carly exclaimed, "Kristin! What a surprise!"

I couldn't decide whether to laugh or cry. My eyes slid from Carly to the two sheepish-faced people standing next to her: Melanie and James.

Melanie looked stricken. "Sorry," she mouthed as James shook his head in disgust.

"What are you guys doing here?" I tried to sound natural, like this was just a typical coincidence on a typical Saturday morning.

"I love the farmer's market." Carly waved past me. "Drew, is that you?"

Fake. Faker. Fakest.

In a second, she was at his side. In two seconds, she had launched into an idea for the catalog, something about using hydroponics to grow tomatoes in greenhouses in the winter and how growing plants in water increases the yield and *"wouldn't that be a unique and interesting addition to offer along with the catalog greenhouse?"*

As if the average family wanted a hundred tomatoes every week instead of ten. She didn't actually use those numbers, but the point is, well...the point is, really, that Carly is just one big, brown-nosing, jealous faker.

"We were at work and suddenly she started to talk about coming here. We tried to talk her out of it," Melanie whispered.

James leaned toward me. "But when she said she was going to *make an opportunity happen,* that's when we decided we'd better come, too. To stop her from doing whatever that meant."

"Obviously we failed."

"Obviously." I watched Carly talking animatedly, hands waving as she discussed natural growing techniques. It was fascinating to hear the woman who regularly made sarcastic remarks about my garden on the roof pretending to have a deep interest in farming.

"I'd be happy to get the information to you on Monday," she was saying.

Melanie and I each pushed a finger into our chin.

"Is she always like that?" Drew asked once the other three were gone.

We passed a booth filled with fresh flowers—some in bouquets and some not—daisies, hydrangeas, sunflowers, zinnias, roses, snapdragons—all standing upright in large white buckets.

"Like what?" I bent to inhale the scents that had mingled into a lovely, soothing fragrance.

"On. Is she always *on* like that?"

I hesitated, not sure how much to say. "Carly...knows what she wants and goes for it."

"Ambitious."

"That's a nice way of putting it." I stopped in front of a bucket filled with red, yellow, and orange snapdragons.

"These are my favorite. My grandma used to grow snapdragons in the bed between her house and the driveway. All along the side of this house was such a beautiful mass of colors. She's the person who taught me about gardens."

"I'm sorry she's gone," Drew said.

"Oh, she's not. Sorry. She's in a condominium. After my grandpa died, she only stayed in the house a few years." I brought a snapdragon up to my nose. "Did you know some snapdragons are really fragrant and some hardly smell at all?"

"Kind of like people. Metaphorically speaking."

I couldn't help but think of Carly.

"To tell you the truth, I didn't even know what kind of flowers these were." He lifted a snapdragon bunch out of one of the buckets, water dripping from the end of each stem, and paid the woman behind the counter. Then he held the flowers out to me. "For your grandmother."

I was so surprised I didn't take them. "What if she lives in California?"

"Does she?"

A delighted laugh slipped out of me, nurtured by Drew's thoughtfulness. Grandma would love these flowers. She would reminisce about gardens and Grandpa and raising their family. She would talk about how much she loves her grandchildren—and how they should all hurry up and get married. And as a diehard romantic, she'd adore how I got them and insist that today's research trip was surely the start of a love story.

I shook my head. "No. She lives nearby."

"Well, then, give them to her."

"But what if she really did live in California?"

He tilted his head back and looked up at the clear sky. "Then I would tell you to keep them so you can be reminded of her whenever you're at home. It would be all good memories, right?"

"All great memories." My throat tightened. "Thank you." I took the flowers and purposely sent my gaze over the crowds in the next aisle in a futile effort at keep myself from thinking of Drew as anything more than the president of The Joneses.

Someone ducked behind the narrow tent pole of the fresh picked corn stand, and I let out a quiet snort of derision. As if a six-inch tent pole could hide a person. I squinted to see better. My jaw dropped.

Allie?

ELEVEN

ALLIE LEANED AROUND THE TENT POLE AND GAVE A GUILTY wave with an ear of corn.

A break in the crowd opened up my line of sight and I spotted Megan and Bree pretending to be engrossed in filling a paper bag with ears of corn.

Seriously? Everyone had come to spy this morning?

Allie nudged Bree and whispered something in her ear. Bree looked in my direction, grinning like the cat that swallowed the canary. She pointed a quick finger at Drew, who was, thankfully, engrossed in testing homemade jam on water crackers, then made the a-okay sign with her thumb and forefinger. I shifted slightly to hide my face in case Drew glanced my way, then glared at her.

"Okay, okay," she mouthed as my phone dinged with a text.

Flowers tight in the crook of my arm, I swiped the

screen with my thumb to open a message from Bree: *We just wanted to see what he looked like.*

My phone dinged again and I read from Allie: *He's taller than Nate.*

Another ding sounded. From Bree: *Can we meet him?*

Okay, that was as far as this was going to go.

"What's going on?" Drew asked, suddenly next to me.

My heart thumped. "Can you hold these a second?" I handed him the bouquet of flowers. "I have a...little business issue."

"Something with The Joneses?"

The heat prickling on my back combusted into fire. I couldn't say *yes*—he might ask questions and figure out I was lying. "Ah...no. For Get Outa Town," I said in a too-high voice. "Sorry."

Drew went over to try the cucumber samples at the next stand while I sent a reply: *No you can't meet him. It's not a date, remember?*

Before I could even put my phone away, it dinged again. Bree: *He's cuter than Nate.*

Ding! Allie: *I could watch him eat those cucumber slices all day.*

I fired off a reply: *He's my boss, sicko.*

Ding! Allie: *Sicko? I'm mortally wounded.*

Ding! Bree: *You need to find out if he has a girlfriend.*

Ding! Allie: *When's the last time you saw a cucumber slice go into a mouth that beautiful? Just saying.*

Ding! Bree: If he's single, maybe today could turn into a date.

Ding! Allie: Now he's eating pie. Heaped with whipped cream. I'm dying.

I pivoted to see Drew across the aisle at Farm Fresh Pies—best pies in the world if you ask me. He took a bite of pie, then used his finger to wipe whipped cream off his upper lip. And then—I watched, transfixed, as if it was a movie—he stuck his finger in his mouth and sucked off the whipped cream. I could totally understand what the girls were saying.

Ding! I started so badly I almost dropped my phone. A text from Bree: *When life gives you lemons, make lemonade.*

What?

Ding! Allie: Looks like the continental breakfast gods delivered!

Ding! Megan: Shut off your phone before these two drive me crazy.

Her and me both.

As for the continental breakfast gods? So far, it looked like all they'd delivered to me was chaos. But then I saw Drew eating pie and holding that bouquet of flowers for my Grandmother, and my chest swelled with emotion. I put my phone on silent and shoved it into my purse.

"Okay, that's fixed," I chirped to Drew. "She got mixed up about which restaurant she was supposed be at."

We started to walk again, and Drew handed me the flowers. "You're not the only reviewer?"

I pictured my photo on the header of the site. Stupid me. Stupid us. We'd set up the blog as being mine alone. Just me. "No, no, I mean, yes. It's my site, I do the reviews. But I asked a friend to...retake some pictures for me. The ones I took were too dark, and one of the things I'm really particular about is making sure the places I review look good. It helps build goodwill. With the restaurants, I mean." Too much, just shut up already.

"How do you decide which restaurants to review? Other than being accosted by complete strangers at breakfast?"

This blog site was, apparently, going to be the bane of my existence for the rest of my life. Or at least until the day I took it down. "Word of mouth mostly. Someone tells me about a restaurant, or I read about a new opening..."

"I was hoping you'd say that. There's this new restaurant downtown, Maisey's."

"I haven't heard of it."

"Yeah," he said on an exhale. "The chef is a friend of my brother's. They were in culinary school together."

I nodded and waited, afraid to find out where he was going with this.

"She's really talented. The food is amazing."

"Let me guess. They'd be a great place to review," I said, faking a smile. I was so sick of Get Outa Town, I could scream.

Drew shrugged apologetically. "Nate asked me to

mention it. Said to ask you if lobbying with a few dozen donuts would help influence your decision."

Just what I needed, more Grandad's Donuts. I hadn't gotten on a scale in two weeks because I was terrified of what I would see. "It's tempting. But I don't accept gifts so no one can ever say I was bribed to give a good review," I said, making up rules on the fly. "But I'll put Maisey's on my list."

Of course I would. If a review would make the president of The Joneses happy, a review was what he would get.

I pointed to a large stand at the end of the aisle and happily changed the subject. "There's Friendly Frank's. See the guy in the black t-shirt with the black cowboy hat? That's Frank. I told him we'd be stopping today."

After introducing the two men, I waited an appropriate length of time—five minutes, to be exact—before interrupting their conversation to take my leave. "Excuse me, guys. Hey, I'm sorry to interrupt, but Drew, I have to take off. I've got some other things to do today." The dogs at the animal shelter were waiting for their walks. And the girls and I needed to brainstorm ideas for Nate's booth at *Taste of Twin Cities*.

"Good, okay, listen Kristin, that review we were talking about—how about tomorrow night?"

It took me a second to process his words. Then my stomach flopped, half irritation, half anticipation. Just because he wanted to help a friend, and just because he was the company president, didn't mean he had the right dictate what I did in my time off and when I did it. "Tomorrow night?" I asked evenly. "I wasn't—"

"I thought it might help if I went, too. Introduce you to the chef...without telling her you're a reviewer, of course. The rest of my week is booked solid. I'll be out of town for a few days, so tomorrow night's the best I have."

Drew wanted to go with me? This was ridiculous. I didn't even really do reviews. I drew a deep breath. He'd probably ask a ton of questions about my process, which meant I'd have to create a process before then in order to fake him out.

Besides, I had Sunday family dinner at Grandma's. Although she was always understanding if any of us had other commitments.

"Um, let me check my calendar," I said, stalling to gain a few seconds to think. I opened the calendar on my phone and perused my empty schedule.

I opened my mouth to tell him I had other plans when it suddenly dawned on me that Opportunity—with a capital O—had just jumped into my lap. I knew how the world worked—*you scratch my back, I'll scratch yours.* Drew held the future of my job in the palm of his hand. He could fire me. He could promote me.

He could kiss me.

I colored slightly at the thought. Oh, for God's sake.

Drew raised his eyebrows, waiting.

I frantically scrolled through the next month's calendar so it appeared that I was looking at a very busy schedule and asked myself, *Should I or shouldn't I?*

He wanted to help a friend's business—and I presented an opportunity for him to do that. If I was smart, this could be an opportunity for me, too. Like that old saying: *when opportunity knocks and wants to scratch your back, let it.* Or something like that.

Grandma would totally understand about me missing dinner. "That sounds great," I said. "What time?"

As I sped away from the farmer's market, my brain was like a cursor bouncing over a row of emoji faces trying to choose the right expression—happy, surprised, excited, worried, sad, scared, winky, tongue sticking out, dizzy...

To be perfectly honest, I didn't know what I was feeling, only that from the minute I met Drew Lawson, my life had been twisting and turning in ways I would never have anticipated.

I screeched into a parking space at the animal shelter and spotted Allie, Megan, and Bree cooling their heels on a bench near the entryway. Though they were trying to look angry, they couldn't hold back their grins.

Twenty minutes later, with two dogs leashed and

happy, the four of us were charging down the sidewalk, everyone talking at once.

"I think Drew may like you," Allie said. "Something in his body language just says *attracted*."

"Come on, he's my boss." I walked faster, swinging my arms to disperse the thrill that cavorted through me at her words. "But I'll entertain the idea." I accidentally tugged back on the leash of the dog I was walking, and he stopped as though I had given him a command. "Sorry, sorry." I urged him forward as I turned to Bree and said. "Specifics, please."

"We were watching the two of you for way longer than you know," Bree said. "We saw the salsa chip moment."

"We also saw the way he handed you that strawberry," Allie chipped in.

"Which strawberry?" I didn't remember that as a particularly romantic moment.

"The one with chocolate on it. Everyone knows that chocolate-covered strawberries symbolize romance."

"The woman working at the stand handed it to me—not Drew."

"And he gave you flowers," Bree added, ignoring me. "A full bouquet."

"*To give to my grandmother.*" These were the signs of attraction they'd spotted?

I threw a disbelieving look at Megan.

"Don't think I'm part of this," she said. "You know I

don't believe in Cinderella stories. I went to the farmer's market because I'm reviewing it for the blog. But our other friends," She nodded at Allie and Bree who had the good sense to appear chagrined, "thought they were undercover agents on a spy mission."

"It wasn't a spy mission," Bree protested. "We just wanted to see what he looked like. After all, once upon a time at continental breakfast, Kristin thought he was a pretty handsome guy."

"Yes, when I thought he was a security guard. And then I lied to him. And ditched him. And discovered he was the new president at my job." I threw my hands in the air, shaking the leash attached to the dog I was walking yet again. "Now, it's hard to see him as anything other than the guy who could ruin my life if he discovered everything I've done to deceive him." I scrubbed a hand over my face. "And despite all that, sometimes I do picture him as... something more and then hate myself for it."

"Maybe it'll be easier when Get Outa Town slides into the background," Allie said.

I shook my head. "Maybe it won't. I have another fifteen more followers. And get this—I got an email this morning from some advertising company that wants to put ads on the blog and pay me for the privilege."

All three swiveled toward me, mouths gaping.

"Seriously?" Allie asked.

"Did you check them out?" Megan added.

I nodded. "Totally legit. I—we'll—get paid for every impression—that's whenever someone sees an ad. And we'll make even more every time someone clicks on one."

"Hard to argue with cash." Bree gave me a thumbs up. "Did you give them the go-ahead?"

"Of course. Even if we don't make any money, ads will make the site authentic."

"Maybe Get Outa Town is destined for the big time," Allie said.

"I hope not. Minor success is already bringing a new set of problems." I brushed my hair back. "Drew asked me to do a review for a restaurant owned by some friend of Nate's."

The girls murmured sympathetically.

"Even worse, he wants to come along. Seems to think if he introduces me to the chef, I can get a better review somehow."

"He wants to come along?" Bree squealed. "That's not *even worse*. I'm not sure what it is, but it's not *even worse*."

Megan sighed. "It's also not *even better*. We could beat this dead horse all day and nothing would change. Let's put the fairytale out of the way and get to business. Kristin, you said you wanted some help today?" she puffed out as we strode up a steep hill, two-by-two with the dogs in the lead.

"Yeah. Nate's looking for ideas to make his booth stand out at *Taste of Twin Cities*."

"Free samples would do it for me," Bree said. "Lots of free samples."

"He's doing that already. What else can I suggest that would bring people to his stand? And don't say, have a face painter." I shortened my steps to make the hill climb easier.

"A donut decorating table for kids," Allie exclaimed. "Give them plain cake donuts that they can customize with different frostings and toppings, like jimmies and sprinkles and berries."

Megan frowned. "It would probably break health department codes for food service. You know...open containers, kids' dirty hands."

"Great idea for a birthday party," I said. "For a crowd of thousands, maybe not so much."

"Have you seen those wedding cakes made out of donuts?" Bree chimed in. "He could offer those."

"At Taste of Twin Cities?"

"The rules of brainstorming say there's no such thing as a bad idea," Bree said a little defensively.

"You're right. Donut wedding cakes are definitely a thought."

Bree pointed a finger at me. "I know what you're doing! *That's a thought* is just a nice way of saying *no*," she said, repeating the words I'd said to her the morning of The Joneses company meeting.

"Girls, focus. His selling point is really the donuts,"

Megan said. "At *Taste of Twin Cities*, it's going to be all about having enough samples."

"I think you're right," I said. "What would make you buy a Grandad's Donut? Someone painting a bumblebee on your kid's cheek? Or the most delicious sample you've ever tasted"

"It wouldn't hurt to have a couple of donut cakes on display in the booth. And a picture in the flyer," Bree pointed out. "That, and a birthday party donut decorating kit—"

"Agreed. As long as the flyer hasn't been printed already. Money sounds really tight." I twisted my mouth. "And I doubt he can afford to reprint it a third time."

"Maybe he should ask his rich brother for a loan," Allie said.

No one said anything for a long beat.

"Speaking of his rich brother..." Bree pulled off her sweatshirt and tied it around her waist. "I'm thinking he has two reasons for going on this review with you. One has to do with reviewing the restaurant—and the other has to do with reviewing you."

"You mean, to see if I should get laid off or not."

She looked at me like I was a dimwit and shook her head. "Not laid off. Laid. I think it's to see if you should get laid or not."

Megan, Allie, and I started screeching, which scared the dogs into barking, which then effectively ended the conversation, thank God.

~

"Do you have a procedure you follow when doing a review?" Drew asked.

Sitting across from him in the low light of the cozy restaurant triggered some of the same panic I experienced when he confronted me at continental breakfast two weeks ago. I reined in my fear and tried to remember that he was just a guy who wanted me to do a review for friend; at this moment, he wasn't my boss and, despite what Allie and Bree wanted to believe, he sure wasn't a date.

Even though he would be one fine date to see across the table. Just saying.

I shook my napkin into my lap. "Typically I order a lot of food, a few appetizers and two or three main dishes, so I always appreciate having someone along to help eat it."

He grinned. "Happy to oblige."

"It also helps to have someone along so it's not obvious what I'm doing. Throughout the meal, I'll be filling out a form I created—on my phone—with ratings and comments about the food, service, décor, and ambience." Luckily, I had spent some time earlier in the day working up a reviewing method so everything would seem authentic.

"And when do you write the review?"

"Whenever I have some free time. This one, though, I'll do right away."

The waiter brought out our drinks, a craft beer I'd

never heard of for Drew and glass of Malbec for me, then re-lit the candle on our table as we placed an order for three appetizers. "To great reviews," Drew said and tapped his glass against mine. "What score would you give the atmosphere in here?"

"It's wonderful. Comfortable, romantic, really appealing. Probably a five out of five." I took a swallow of wine and then another, welcoming its warm glide down my throat.

"I like it, too. Reminds me of a place I used to go to in New York."

"This move has to be a big change for you. Do you miss being there?"

Drew considered the question. "Parts of it, yeah. But not all. Not my job. When I got out of school, I thought investment banking was my path to...everything that mattered. Great pay, impressive responsibilities..."

"And it wasn't?"

Amusement flitted across his face and disappeared. "That great pay? Once you figure in grueling eighteen-hour workdays, you realize your hourly wage isn't all that great. Then, you have to figure in the cost of no time for a personal life." He shoved a hand through his hair. "Don't get me wrong. I knew it would be hard, but I didn't care because I thought I could make a difference."

Confused, I narrowed my eyes. Make a difference on Wall Street? Was he serious or was this a business joke that I didn't get, kind of like the latest business jargon.

He took a drink of beer. "Sounds ridiculous, right? I thought I'd be able to get into socially-responsible investing. Or...maybe if I helped big companies save money, they'd pass some of their savings down to their customers. I just expected that, working in the financial industry I'd be able to make a positive contribution to society."

I was so dumbfounded by his expectation, I couldn't think of anything to say.

The candle flickered out again, sending a thin stream of smoke wafting up from the wick.

He gave me a lopsided smile. "A lot of people who go from college to Wall Street arrive there hoping to make a difference. The dream dies more slowly for some than for others. Four years into the job, my boss called me in and laid it on the line. He said, *We're here to make money, not save the world.* That was the beginning of the end for me, although I didn't realize it at the time." He picked up the unlit candle. "It's like this...you can keep relighting the wick, but eventually you realize that you're better off just getting a new candle."

I tried to wrap my head around what he'd just said. Drew was a save the world kind of guy? Despite my insistence that tonight's dinner was nothing more than two people doing a restaurant review, suddenly it took all my willpower to hold back my attraction to him. "It must have been awful staying there."

"I just buried my expectations and kept going, making

money for the company. Took another four years and a failed relationship before I figured out that Wall Street and I weren't a good match." He paused for a long beat. "Sorry. You're probably thinking, *damn, why did I agree to let this guy come along tonight*?"

If he only knew the truth. "Actually, I was thinking, damn, this guy is a lot more interesting than I expected him to be."

He threw back his head and laughed. "I think that's a compliment."

"And I was also thinking the catalog will be better off for having you." My cheeks started to pink at that sudden burst of honesty and I took a quick sip of wine.

"I hope you're right. So how did you come to work at The Joneses?"

Ugh. I gave my standard reply, putting a positive spin on my stint as a merchandising assistant, and how I'd been promised a promotion to assistant buyer when I came on board, but the department had never grown the way it had been predicted.

Drew didn't say anything to that, and I decided to shut up before he concluded I was an ungrateful whiner. Luckily, the waiter arrived to see three exquisite platters of appetizers on our table and relight the candle.

I put some bacon wrapped dates on my plate, and Drew helped himself to a piece of smoked salmon tartine and grilled tomato bread. "If everything tastes as good as it looks, could be five stars," I said, hoping to redirect our conversation.

"You know, I never got your answer to the question I asked my first day," Drew said around a bite of appetizer. "Remember that? What do you think is the catalog's greatest strength and weakness?"

I felt a spasm of unease. My fear about sounding like a whiner five minutes ago quadrupled. The last thing I wanted was to be critical. He had already set the company's direction; there was no need for me to harp upon a different path—even if I thought it was a better one. After all, I wasn't saving the world anymore.

All I needed to say was what he wanted to hear—that I believed he and the board made the right decision. So easy. I tilted my head to give the impression that I was thinking through my answer. Then I repeated exactly what I'd said that first morning, the company line: "Our strength is our innovative product mix that appeals to people's basic need to feel like they've arrived."

"And our weakness?" he asked, apparently accepting my first answer without question.

I bit my tongue. Oh, I had such an opinion about this, but no way could I share it. I took a fortifying swallow of wine and said in a light voice, "Isn't that what you hired all the experts for?" I mentally patted myself on the back for sidestepping the question so neatly.

The slight flicker in Drew's eyes made me think he was wondering whether the reason I hadn't ever moved up the ladder was because I wasn't capable. Maybe I shouldn't have answered so flippantly.

"The experts haven't been working there for four years. You have." He leaned forward like an interrogator, certain I was withholding information that he was determined to get. The thought unnerved me, and I glanced away hoping to see the waiter coming back to take our dinner order.

Stalling, I chomped down on a date. I couldn't afford to step out of line. With everything that was going on at The Joneses, I needed to keep a low profile, my nose to the grindstone, my eyes on the long picture, and my words from offending anyone.

"No opinion?" He sat back in his chair.

Oh, great, a trick question. If I said I had no opinion, I sounded like an employee who just collects her paycheck. But if I admitted I had thoughts on the issue, I was going to have to share them—and my ideas didn't exactly align with the current direction of the catalog.

"Well, no. Um, I mean, yes," I stammered stupidly. I held my breath hoping it was enough.

Was there any wonder that his brows pulled together? He was probably thinking he'd seriously overestimated my intelligence level.

And, truthfully, at that point I was beginning to think the same thing.

"It's okay if you don't care," Drew said. "I get it. Sometimes a job is just a job."

My heart rate sped up. It was hard to ignore the fact that he was probably forming a not-very-flattering opinion about me: *No dedication. Certainly not management material.*

My dreams of a new job were likely evaporating with every bite of appetizer I swallowed.

"Why does it matter?" I asked. "Isn't the catalog's direction already cast in stone?"

"You're right. The direction was set before I came on board," he said around a mouthful of appetizer. "But I've always thought they should have queried the employees, the people in the trenches, to get their point of view. So I'm doing it now. I think knowing what bugs people, what they think could be improved, will make us stronger."

The president of The Joneses valued me for more than just delivering coffee?

All my ideas for the catalog surged to the front of my mind. How could it hurt to tell him what I thought? Maybe he'd find my ideas helpful, maybe he'd love what I had to say and I'd be promoted to a higher level position within the week. A shot of adrenalin made me shiver. What if the very ideas that could save the catalog were...mine?

I knew it sounded a bit grandiose, but what if? Seriously, *what if?*

Which is why I decided to let *save the world* out of its cage for this conversation. I'd tell Drew exactly what I thought, after which I would lock away my helping gene once more—and this time throw away the key for real.

"So... I actually don't think our product mix is the catalog's greatest strength," I blurted out in a too-high voice. Drew looked taken aback. Maybe he was just surprised at how fast the words rocketed out of me.

I paused a second to grab hold of my thoughts and slow my delivery. No need to seem a little crackers when proposing ideas that ran counter to everyone in charge. "To be honest, I'm not sure what our greatest strength is. But I think I know how to overcome our greatest weakness."

TWELVE

Drew nodded at me to continue. He reached for some grilled tomato bread.

"Bottom line, our greatest weakness is low sales. And I think we overcome that by changing the overall look and feel of the catalog—not by doubling down on pages of super expensive...stuff. The catalog needs to become an experience, a source of inspiration—something people won't want to throw away."

As I warmed to the subject, my words came faster, my voice rose with enthusiasm, and I sat straighter in my chair. "The Joneses should be something people look forward to getting. With beautiful photo spreads, adventure articles, inspirational stories that draw people in and keep them turning the pages. That connection will generate sales."

Drew nodded. "It's a really interesting premise. I have

to admit I was intrigued when I first heard it."

"You heard it already?" I could hardly get the words out. "Where?"

"Carly mentioned it last week. Said she'd been thinking about it a long time."

My mouth froze in a circle of surprise. Carly had taken credit for a concept I came up with six months ago? And now Drew thought I was stealing the idea from her? I didn't know what to say. How would it go down if I accused her of theft? I was a merchandising assistant; she was on her way to a vice presidency.

"Carly told you...about...it?" My brain was scrolling back through the past year—to a departmental lunch where I'd enthusiastically shared the idea. Carly had called me idealistic and said I needed to get a better handle on how the business world actually worked.

He nodded. "I told her to work up a quick proposal with examples and costs. She seems to be pretty sharp."

A lot of adjectives describing Carly came to mind at that moment and sharp was not one of them. I clenched my hands together in my lap to contain my anger. At least I hadn't spilled all my ideas for the catalog that day.

"There's more to it than just changing the catalog's look," I said evenly. "With all due respect, I don't think the answer is to offer bigger, better, more expensive toys for the ultra-rich. Uh, sorry, I mean people with unlimited disposable income."

I was so angry about Carly, I didn't wait for him to

respond, just barreled forward. "The catalog should be going in the opposite direction—from conspicuous consumption to inconspicuous consumption." I took a swallow of wine.

"What do you mean?"

"I've read studies about how acquiring possessions delivers only a temporary boost in happiness. The thrill doesn't last. People are coming to realize that owning more stuff is just...owning more stuff. That buying one thing after another doesn't satisfy the basic human need to feel like our lives matter."

Drew set his elbows on the table and steepled his hands. "Go on."

Heartened, I pushed forward. "Life seems to be getting harder. We're not getting along with each other. We're all trying to keep up with The Joneses." I made a face. "Bad pun. But here's what's really cool. The same research that shows that possessions don't deliver lasting happiness, also shows that helping, making a difference in the lives of others, does."

Come to think of it, that might go a long way toward explaining my save the world predisposition.

"Assuming that's true...what does it have to do with the catalog?"

I put my hands on the table and leaned forward. "We give the catalog a new *brand*. Not just a fresh look and feel, but also a product offering that makes it easier for people to be better human beings. Things like..."

I scrambled to come up with an example. "Well, there's a different catalog that lets people to buy a cow or a goat for a family in an impoverished country. I'm not saying we would do that, it's just an example, but..." My thoughts stumbled, squeezed between the pressure to deliver on the spot and the fact that I'd never fully fleshed out the idea.

I took a couple of sips of wine to buy some time. "Oh! So, for example, customers might be able to pay for a portion of a deep well to bring fresh water to an area that doesn't have any. The catalog would also have a story in it about a country where this was done, and the impact it made on peoples' lives. Pictures, stories, graphs." I gestured with one hand. "From the layout to the product mix, The Joneses brand should be as a source of items that...enlighten, motivate, and inspire."

Drew was staring at me like he couldn't quite believe the words coming from my mouth, and it dawned on me that he might well think I was a woo-woo wacko. Which caused even more words to tumble out in my quest to sound rational. "It's like that lesson we all learned in kindergarten—share, care, and cooperate—which we somehow lose sight of on the path to fame, fortune, and success. And then everyone wonders why they feel so unfulfilled. Why life doesn't seem to have meaning."

"Share, care, and cooperate. Enlighten, motivate, inspire. Sure would bring new meaning to the phrase, *Keeping up with the Joneses*." He sharpened his gaze on me. "Do you have the studies that back this up?"

"I can get them." I was so thrilled at his response, I could have jumped up and down.

"Good." He tipped up his beer glass. "And here I thought you were going to say our greatest weakness was low catalog distribution...which is more or less what everyone else said. Nice thinking outside the box."

A compliment from someone at The Joneses? I almost veered into giddy shock.

The sudden ringing of my cellphone brought me back to the moment. "Sorry. I forgot to shut it off." I retrieved the phone from my purse and spotted my grandmother's number on the screen.

Oh, shit. I took those snapdragons over to her yesterday and forgot to say I wouldn't be at dinner tonight. "Just a second," I said, holding up my index finger. "Hey Gram."

"Sweetheart, we're nearly ready to eat," Gram said." Are you almost here?"

I tightened my grip on the phone. "I'm really sorry, Grandma, I forgot to tell you I had other plans tonight."

"You can't come?" I could feel her disappointment through the phone.

"I'll be there next Sunday for sure." I threw an apologetic smile at Drew.

"Is this because of the same project you were working on last weekend?"

I nodded even though she couldn't see me. "We have a lot to get done. And deadlines are coming up."

"Even if you're working, you still have to eat."

A whimper formed in my throat. This wasn't going as easily as I had hoped it would. "Don't worry, we'll eat."

"I made two full pans of lasagna. What will I do with all these leftovers?" she fretted. "Three loaves of French bread. Why don't you bring your project people along with you?"

Panic stirred my stomach. "Oh, we couldn't Gram, we're so—"

"How many people are there?"

I hesitated. "One."

Drew was eating appetizers and watching me with great interest.

"Just one? Oh my goodness. Of course, bring her—him—which is it?"

"Uh, it's...him."

"It's a man," she said in a muffled voice, probably because she was covering the mouthpiece with her hand so she could announce the news to my entire family. Then she was back. "Kristin, honey, just bring him with you. You don't have to stay long. Eat and run, we don't care."

No way in hell. The last thing I needed was Drew to mention GetOutaTown.com to my family. I could just see them asking what it was and me trying to explain why I'd kept my blog secret and him beginning to wonder what the truth was. "Oh, Gram, he won't want to. It's important business—"

"If I know you, you're working so hard you're putting

off eating to get more done. He's probably starving, poor man. Let me talk to him."

What? Nervous energy skidded up my spine. Who knew what my grandmother would say once she had Drew on the phone. "You don't need to talk to him."

Drew reached out his right hand as if he expected me to pass him the phone. I shook my head.

"Just give him the phone, honey," my grandmother insisted as though I was a four-year-old who wouldn't share.

Drew wiggled the fingers on his outstretched hand. Shit, the president of the company, the boss of all bosses, wanted my phone. Did I even have a choice in this? "My grandmother," I said in weak resignation as I handed over my phone.

Drew put the phone to his ear and said, "Hi, I'm Drew."

I took a bacon-wrapped date, shoved it in my mouth, and waited for the other shoe to drop, the eye of the tornado to pass, the volcano to blow, the freight train that was my grandmother to drive through the station without stopping.

After a pause, Drew said, "This is totally my fault. I pushed Kristin to do this tonight. I didn't know she had other plans—"

"It's not mandatory attendance every week," I leaned toward him and hissed. "I just forgot to tell her."

After a moment, he let out a chuckle. "Actually, I love lasagna."

Of course he did.

My life was disintegrating before my eyes.

"This is awfully nice of you. Sure, sure, it's all right with me. Kristin and I can finish this project another time."

Oh. My. God.

"Okay, then, see you soon." Drew shut off my phone and handed it back. "She really wants you to come to dinner tonight."

Not just me, I muttered silently. It's not just me she wants over there.

Our arrival at my grandmother's felt a little like a television holiday commercial. You know, the long-absent family members arriving at the homestead to cries of happiness, joyous hugs, and heartfelt kisses. All we needed was some snow, a Christmas tree, and the song Silver Bells playing in the background and the scene would have been complete.

In the middle of the introductions, Adam threw me a knowing grin. I rolled my eyes in reply as if to say, *What's the big deal?* In reality, though, I was a bundle of nervous energy, still trying to figure out how I had managed to go from introducing Drew to Farmer Frank, to bringing Drew to Sunday night family dinner.

I looked at Ethan and Heather. "Home two weekends in a row. What's up with that?"

"We miss you," Ethan said.

"He has a meeting in St. Paul tomorrow," Heather added.

I snorted out a laugh and exchanged a look with Bree. She slid over to my side and whispered. "Well, this is interesting. I thought you were going to cancel."

"I forgot."

Grandma clapped her hands a couple of times. "Everyone to the table. Let's eat before the food gets cold." She hustled us into the dining room where the snapdragons from Drew had been artfully arranged in a clear vase at the center of the table.

Oh God, please don't let her bring up the flowers.

"The flowers are from a friend of Kristin's. Aren't they beautiful?" Grandma said. "Honey, did you thank your friend for me?"

Uggggh. I nodded. "Those are from Drew, Gram." I wiggled a finger weakly in his direction. "He bought them for you."

"You're the one? Oh, Drew, thank you. Snapdragons are my favorites." Grandma gave him a hug, her face alight with joy.

"Drew got flowers for Grandma?" Ethan asked under his breath.

"I think we're missing something here," Adam said as he took a seat next to Bree. "Kristin?"

Oh, this was just not going well. I ignored them and slid stiffly into a chair at the table.

Only once everyone's plates were full and the

conversation flowing, did I begin to relax. I'd made a point of introducing Drew as The Joneses' new president, hoping that would be enough to keep my family from asking any questions. They knew how long I'd been angling for a better job, so I knew none of them would risk saying anything that might inadvertently hurt my chances. Which meant our conversation stayed on safe topics, such as the weather, the upcoming professional football season, and vacations (both previous and upcoming).

Everything was going along fine, albeit somewhat superficial, when Grandma asked, "Are you married, Drew?"

Mortification sent a rush of color to my cheeks. Ethan tossed an understanding frown my way; he'd been the recipient of Grandma's steady matchmaking until his recent marriage.

Drew took it in stride. "No. Working eighteen hour days in New York didn't leave a lot of time for romance."

"Maybe you'll have more time now that you're in Minnesota."

A long moment passed, silence stretching from one end of the table to the other.

"So, Drew," Adam said, and I knew he was going to change the subject. My brothers are the greatest, even if they're obnoxious sometimes. "After all those years in high finance, do you have any tips for the rest of us?"

"Preferably of the get rich quick variety," Bree added.

Grandma nodded. "That's right. Some of us don't have that many years left to watch our money grow."

"Gram!" my mom said.

"Or even to see our great grandchildren grow up." Grandma looked around the table, the soft skin of her cheeks creasing from her smile.

Ethan laughed. "You don't even have any great grandchildren yet."

"Yes, but at least now I have hope since some of you have taken a step in the right direction by tying the knot."

Heather put a hand over her mouth to smother an escaping chortle.

Grandma turned to Drew as she took a second helping of lasagna. "Ethan and Heather got married last month at the ocean. They've known each other for years, but the wedding was a marvelous surprise. My husband and I, on the other hand, only knew each other for three weeks when we married—"

"And it lasted for sixty years," Ethan, Adam, and I said in unison.

"Sixty wonderful years," Grandma said, paying us no attention. "Would you like some more lasagna, Drew?" Without waiting for his answer, she scooped a slice from the pan and set it on his plate.

"Mom, you didn't give him time to reply," my dad said.

"He could use a few more pounds." Grandma put a slice of French bread on his plate and pushed the butter dish toward him. "He's too thin. Eat all you want, Drew."

"Gram, he's perfect the way he is," I burst out in Drew's defense, figuring he would be too polite to say anything back in this roomful of strangers.

Adam grinned, and Ethan slanted an amused sideways glance my way. I exhaled slowly, realizing immediately their concern. In my quest to rescue Drew, I had essentially announced I thought he was the perfect male specimen. Gram would be all over this in seconds.

A blush rose up my cheeks. "What I meant was—" I couldn't even look at Drew. "That he doesn't need to gain weight, that he—" I furiously sought some way to finish the sentence. "—should just eat whatever he wants and not feel forced into it because he doesn't know everyone here."

"And I definitely want more." Drew put a forkful of lasagna into his mouth, whisking away the moment's awkwardness. "It's delicious. Is this an old family recipe?"

"Yes," Grandma replied, nodding, as Adam said, "Yeah, straight out of the Betty Crocker Cookbook."

Grandma gave Adam a disapproving once-over. "It's the Good Housekeeping Cookbook," she said with a sniff. "But I'd like to point out that a recipe doesn't have to be handed down the generations to be an old family recipe. It just has to be beloved. And this one is." She smiled at Drew. "Of course I have my own grandmother's recipe straight from Italy. But who wants to spend all day making tomato sauce when the kind you can buy is delicious. And noodles? Don't even talk to me about how long it takes to make homemade noodles."

"I totally understand," Drew said stabbing a forkful of salad.

Grandma beamed at him. "Do you do any cooking, Drew?"

I nervously wiped my lips with my napkin. Where was she going—

"My late husband wasn't much of a cook, but he did make pancakes," she said.

Oh, no. Not this path. I threw a desperate look at Adam to no avail.

"Used to make mine with a heart-shaped cookie cutter," she finished.

Drew swallowed his mouthful of food. Then he smiled and said, "That's because he knew how lucky he was."

Grandma's eyes glistened. "We both knew," she murmured, extending her hands outward toward all of us at the table. "My greatest joy would be that all of you find that, too."

Then she jumped up to pull an apple pie from the oven —because while she may hate to cook, she loved to bake— and Ethan started talking football again, which led to a friendly argument about which team would go further in the playoffs, and the rest of the dinner proceeded as smoothly as any of our family dinners go. Which is to say, there was rarely a dull moment.

By the time Drew and I left Grandma's, it had begun to rain, a steady stream slightly heavier than drizzle. As Drew walked me to my car, I could feel my hair beginning to kink. "Thanks for coming over here," I said. "It really made my Grandma happy."

"I had fun. Besides, it was the least I could do since I more or less forced you to go to Maisey's tonight."

"Oh, you didn't. Well, not too much, anyway." I got into the driver's seat and opened the window to look up at him. "I like finding out about new places. Helps keep Get Outa Town relevant."

The rain began to fall harder; fat drops slicked down Drew's hair and pattered on my upturned face. Silence opened between us to the point of awkwardness, and I moved to fill it, saying: "I'll go back to Maisey's this week and finish up the review." I wiped the rain off my cheek and grinned. "If the entrees are as good as the appetizers, it's going to be an easy review to write."

He smiled back at me, but didn't leave, his shirt now wet and clinging to his broad chest. Grandma was so wrong; Drew was definitely not too skinny.

Not that I was noticing or anything.

"Sorry about my Grandma going on about...the food," I said.

"The food was delicious," he said. "But I'm more about the company anyway." He put his hands on the open window and bent low, so close that our faces were just inches apart. "And I have to tell you, the company was pretty wonderful."

Lightning split the sky, illuminating him in stark contrast. Rain glimmered in the dark hair on his jaw and he looked a pirate, wet from the sea...and dangerous.

I caught my lip between my teeth. What was going on? Obviously Drew Lawson was incredible. But surely, he wasn't thinking the same thing about me.

Was he?

How could that even be possible?

"You-you're getting wet," I stammered like a moron.

"The view is worth it." he said in complete seriousness.

The view? He was looking at *me*. What was going on here? I mean, really. *What?*

He brushed my wet hair off my forehead. A jolt shot through me just as lightning cracked overhead, and for one ridiculous second I thought I'd been hit by lightning.

Suddenly Drew straightened and stepped away from the car. "Thanks for a great time," he said.

Almost in shock, I nodded and put my car into gear. Giving a little wave, I drove away while he stood in the rain and watched me go.

He was still standing there when I turned the corner.

It was straight out of a movie, and I had no idea what the hell it meant.

THIRTEEN

I woke at five in the morning on the couch, my laptop across my legs and a crick in my neck. Standing, I tried to stretch out the kinks in my back. I'd been so intent on finding the research studies I'd promised to get for Drew, I'd never made it to bed last night.

Fat lot of good staying up late had done me; I still hadn't found what I was looking for.

I stumbled into the shower and headed into work early, hoping I'd bookmarked some of the articles on my work computer. My spirits were high as I strode through the building. Last week, Carly, the idea thief, had been commenting, ad nauseam, about the long hours she'd been putting in. Melanie and I figured she was either showing up early to impress management, or was just so incompetent she needed to put in extra time to keep her head above water with all the tight deadlines. Considering that she'd stolen my idea because she had no good ones of his own, I was putting my money on explanation number two.

Sure enough, there she was at her desk. "Good morning," I said as I strode past.

"Kristin!" she called after me. "Come in here a minute."

"Please?" I prompted, and stopped in the doorway to her office.

"Please what?"

"Never mind. What do you need?"

She pointed to multiple stacks of paper on the floor along the wall.

I stared at them for a second, not catching her point. "Uh, what are those?"

"Hard copies that need to be sorted."

No, no, no. This better not be what it sounded like. I eyed the stacks again. "But where did they come from?"

"My credenza. I don't know what it all is, and I don't have time to figure it out. Some of it goes back to my predecessor. A lot of it may already be saved on the server," she said in a voice too soft and nice to be trusted.

I nodded and took a step back from the doorway to distance myself from what looked to be a truly awful project.

"It's distracting to have these piles in my office." She wrinkled her nose to show her distaste.

"Why don't you put everything back in your credenza to deal with later?"

"Because," she condescended, "I'm working on some specific proposals that Drew wants today. I need you to take charge of this." She waved a hand at the stacks of paper. "Take it all back to your area."

Easy, easy, I warned myself. "And...what happens to it there?"

"You sort it. Check the server to see which pieces are already saved in digital format. Any that aren't need to be filed."

The magnitude of the project hit me like a rotten tomato. Piled together, all those sheets probably made a stack six feet tall. An old expression leapt to mind: if all the paper in Carly's office was laid end-to-end, it would reach around the earth at the equator. Twice.

And I was supposed to sort it all? My chest tightened. "You're kidding, right?" I said. "Because I have other work to do."

"How can this department function smoothly if we don't have order?" Carly spun in her chair and went over to lift a short stack of paper. "Here, I'll help you move it."

Five minutes later, all the sheets were piled in my workspace. "Put this project ahead of everything else," she said, turning to leave. "With all the expectations coming down from the top, I want our department to be ship-shape." Then she reminded me about getting her a large light brown coffee and a chocolate frosted donut from the cart when it came around.

"Ship shape," I said once she was gone, my head ready to explode.

I drew several breaths to calm myself, then began running online searches for the research studies Drew wanted. I quickly found I hadn't bookmarked the articles, but a search of my computer's online history delivered exactly what I was seeking. I grinned at the screen.

Though I was tempted to paste the links into an email and send them to Drew immediately, I held back. I wanted to include examples of products that we could offer in the catalog that would help people make a difference in the lives of others. I wanted examples that were so convincing they would overcome any objections Drew and the board would have to tweaking—or outright changing—the direction of the catalog.

It didn't take me long to create a list. I started with my example from dinner—deep wells to provide safe drinking water—then added piping systems for crop irrigation, supplies for schools, medicine for outpost clinics, lifesaving surgeries for people in need, solar panels for electricity in rural areas...

As the list grew, I began to muse about the impact of this new direction on The Joneses and—oh, finally— maybe even my future. Once everyone knew that I was the person who brought forward his new vision, maybe I could finally begin my upward climb. Manager. Department Head. Director. Assistant Vice President. Vice President. The sky would be my limit—all because I didn't hold back from sharing my ideas about how to fix The Joneses.

My thoughts were interrupted by a call from the director of human resources asking me to come up for a quick meet. Can you imagine? *A quick meet with the director of HR!* Was it possible that Drew had been so impressed by my ideas he decided I should be promoted immediately? I put my arms up and shimmied in my chair. Maybe after learning that I'd never gotten the advancement I'd been promised, he decided it was time for me to climb the ladder.

I knew I was letting my imagination get away from me and tried to control my excitement. But I couldn't help thinking this was a sign that good things were finally coming my way.

"I'll be right up." I stuck out my tongue at the stacks of paper Carly had given me to sort, and charged into the hall.

Ebullient, I took the stairs to the third floor two at a time. I admit, there was a tiny spot in the corner of my brain that entertained the possibility I might be about to lose my job. But I had trouble reconciling that thought with how Drew had acted the night before. Get real. Who would be that wonderful to someone and then hand her a pink slip the next day? Made no sense. This was definitely going to be a celebration-worthy meeting.

The director was a burly man, middle aged and balding. He didn't smile often, and when he did it looked like he was baring his teeth at you. Which is exactly what happened when I tapped on the doorframe of his open door to get his attention. He motioned me to take a seat. *All good signs*, I thought to myself gleefully.

"Kristin, let me say how pleased the company is with the caliber of your work," he said. "You have been reliable, thorough, hard-working..."

Innovative, I said to myself, thinking of the new ideas I'd shared with Drew. *Don't forget innovative.*

"We're glad you're on our team." He did that baring his teeth thing again, then splayed the fingers of both hands on the top of his desk. "So, I'm going to get right to it."

Yes, please do! I was almost levitating with excitement. The first thing I would do with my raise would be to treat Megan, Allie, and Bree to dinner.

"When you were hired, you received an offer letter from The Joneses that spelled out the terms of your employment here. Your signature indicated your agreement with those terms." He tapped a sheet of paper lying on his desk.

I tried to think back four years, to the day I'd been hired, to the moment I signed that agreement. I couldn't remember anything about it other than my salary and number of vacation days. I nodded robot-like, my heart rate beginning to ramp up.

"In it, was a statement, you agreed to—well, here, let me read it to you."

This wasn't sounding like the prelude to a promotion.

He put on wire reading glasses and perused the sheet a moment before reading aloud, "The Joneses considers itself your primary employer and requires full-time attention to your job duties each day. Any outside employment or ownership in any company must be discussed and approved in writing to avoid any potential conflict of interest."

The blood drained from my face. Was this about Get Outa Town?

"It's been brought to my attention that you are the owner of another business called…" He cleared his throat. "Get Outa Town. Is that correct?"

I nodded, unable to speak mostly because I was almost unable to think. I was in trouble over a review website that wasn't even real? How had human resources found out about it? Drew was the only outsider who knew about my blog, and I just couldn't believe he would report me to HR. Not after last night. It didn't make any sense.

"It's not a big deal," I stammered out. "Just a website, a blog actually—"

"Unfortunately, that's not how we see it. You're involved in another business venture, one that's so successful, you have paid advertising on the site."

I should never have said yes to that advertising company. I was going to get reprimanded—or fired—for making a few pennies on the side? My heart seemed to slow to a fraction of its usual rate and time came to a stop.

"I've made a thorough examination of the site, and I

don't see anything that would be a conflict of interest with your job here at The Joneses." He touched the paper again. "As long as you confine your reviews to restaurants and the like...and don't stray into the types of products we offer in the catalog."

As if I could afford to purchase Joneses level products on my salary anyway. "I always intended it to be restaurant reviews only," I said in a steady voice.

If Drew didn't turn me in, then who? It was just the sort of thing I would expect out of Carly, but she'd been totally dismissive of the site that day she spotted it on my computer. Still, what if she'd gone back to the site later? She would realize it was mine the minute she saw my picture on the homepage. I leaned forward. "Did Carly tell you about the site?"

He pursed his lips. "We keep the reporting person's name confidential, so it doesn't cause problems between employees, but...since she's your boss, let me put your fears to rest. It wasn't Carly."

You could have knocked me over with a feather. That left Drew. *Drew.* I couldn't believe it. I had to know. "Was it—?"

"I really can't answer any more questions," he said too quickly. "I already violated policy telling you it wasn't Carly."

If it was Drew, why hadn't he just talked to me? What happened to the man who seemed so interested in my ideas for creating a new, compassionate catalog that helped wealthy people make a difference in the world? The man who said my family was wonderful?

My heart constricted. That man had turned me in?

So what had last night been about then? Why ask me to do a review? Was the whole thing just a setup...a way to find out if I was stealing time from the catalog to work on my review site?

"And as long as you understand that *none* of the activities associated with this business can be conducted during your normal workday."

I shook my head. "Absolutely. No, it's always after hours—"

"Well, that's why I'm talking to you today. We value what you bring to the catalog and would hate to lose you. But rules are rules, and company policy requires me to conduct an investigation. I have some questions for you to answer, and need you to sign a statement agreeing to keep time spent on each job separate, then we'll submit the information to the executive board for discussion and, most likely, approval."

A chill swept over me. All those things Drew said about how cutthroat Wall Street had been, how he'd hated the emphasis on making money at all costs. Yeah right. He hated it so much, he embraced the worst of it and brought it here.

"I promise, it won't be an issue," I said, biting back my bitterness. "Please assure that person I'll take the site down tonight...so there'll be no need to go any further or get any written approvals, and no one can have any doubt about my loyalty to The Joneses."

He smiled. "Well, that certainly takes care of that."

It sure did.

Back at my desk, I perused the information I'd gathered for Drew—all the articles, the links, the details, the product ideas. What a fool I was. An absolute idiot. *When would stupid save the world girl finally accept that nobody was really looking to be saved?*

I closed the file and dragged it to the recycle bin.

When? Why, that would be today. Sometimes it took me a while to learn something, but once I did, I learned it well. From this moment on, I was going to concentrate only on my job duties—and doing my best to stay out of departmental meetings with Drew.

I took a sheaf of pages off the pile I'd gotten from Carly that morning and began the excruciatingly boring task of verifying that a digital version of each existed on the server. Some of them I didn't even have to check—I'd seen the files in the course of working here. My garbage can began to fill with discarded sheets.

Today was the kick in the head that I apparently needed in order to really, truly stop worrying about anything except me. Okay, me, and the dogs at the animal shelter; I couldn't turn my back on them.

"Just wanted you to know that everyone is really pleased with the new product proposals." Drew's voice soared over the top of my six-foot high cubicle walls.

Dread filled me. My *fight or flight* response kicked in and *flight* was about to win. I didn't want to see Drew—not now, not ever.

"Wonderful," Carly said. "I'll share it with the department. Once I got them all working in the right direction, everything seemed to come together."

She and Drew continued talking but their voices grew distant as they moved away from the area. When I couldn't hear them anymore, I let out the breath I was holding.

Not only would Carly never tell us we'd done a good job, but she was already working this so that all credit for the department's efforts ultimately came back to her. Based on what I now knew about Drew, the two of them would get along perfectly.

Or not. What if I was wrong? What if Drew wasn't the person who turned me in? What if someone else knew about the website and I was unfairly blaming Drew? My spirits lifted at the thought.

"What are you so diligently working on?" Melanie appeared in my doorway.

"A project from Carly." I waved a hand at the stacks of paper and explained my new assignment.

Melanie popped her hands onto her hips. "She's jealous."

"Well, we can trade jobs if she wants. She can be

merchandising assistant and I'd be happy to take over as department head."

"No, she's jealous of you and Drew."

I flushed red.

"It's so obvious," Melanie continued. "Drew is listening to your ideas. He's giving you more responsibility. He asked you to meet with him alone last week."

"He's trying to save the catalog. It's not special treatment." *Far from it.*

"Carly's so paranoid about her job, she sees you as a threat. It's the only reason she went to the farmer's market." Melanie dropped into the chair next to my desk and shook her head. "Maybe you should throw all this away, and if anyone ever asks we'll say Carly lost it."

I pushed back in my chair and surveyed the job before me. "Would serve her right."

"I'm not kidding. I bet ninety-nine percent of it is filed somewhere else. Digital or otherwise." Melanie sifted through several sheets. "Most of these I don't even have to check. I know they're on the server because I worked on them." She picked up a stack of papers and began to sort. "I can help for a while."

"You're the best," I said, grinning.

She waved a dismissive hand at me.

An hour later, we were sitting cross legged on the floor, sorting Carly's papers into three piles (retain, discard, or verify). Though we were keeping our energy high with large cups of coffee and Grandad's Donuts, the longer we kept at it, the more my frustration grew. It was hard to believe I could be viewed so differently by the two places I worked. The Joneses saw me as an unrecognizable, someone to handle menial chores, a cheater who was trying to get away with doing two jobs at the same time. While over at Grandad's Donuts, Nate was amazed by my creativity and insight.

"This is scandalous." Melanie threw a couple of sheets onto the small pile of pages that we needed to verify on the server. "Carly kept this disorganized mess in her credenza, yet every year she got recognized with a *Going Above and Beyond the Joneses* award." She folded a sheet into a paper airplane and sent it gliding toward the garbage can. It nosedived into the floor.

I made an airplane out of my next discard page and pushed it out into the airstream. It missed the garbage can, too. Melanie folded another one. I did the same. Mine veered wide and crashed into the wall, but hers flew straight and true, right into the trash.

She pumped her arms up in victory and quietly celebrated, "Safe landing!"

We switched from airplanes to basketball; once a sheet was relegated to the discard pile, we crumpled it into a ball and took aim at the trash can. The game made the project so much more tolerable, we finished the first pile in no time.

I went over to the stacks of paper against the wall and hoisted a pile off the floor, pirouetting toward where

Melanie sat cross legged on the carpet. Not my smartest move. Especially not on a floor covered with paper airplanes and wadded up paper balls. And definitely not while my arms were otherwise engaged and couldn't be used for balance. My right foot landed on an airplane and rocketed forward while my left skidded the other direction. I tried to get my feet underneath me again, but all I succeeded in doing was increasing my downward momentum—and my sense of impending doom.

"Kristin!" Melanie tried to scramble up from the floor.

"Oh fuck!" I landed on the carpet with a thud, my hands flailing upward and shooting papers in every direction.

Breathing hard, I lay on my back on the floor and took in in the disaster around me. White pages lay like giant snowflakes over everything in sight.

Melanie knelt a few steps away, gaping. "Are you okay?

I reached a hand beneath me to rub my lower back. "It looks like a blizzard hit in here."

We started to chortle, one laugh rolling out upon the next. All the tension of the past few weeks slipped out of me. Tears tumbled over my cheeks, and I began to swing my arms and legs like I was lying in a snow-covered yard. "I'm making a snow angel!" I cried as paper scattered in every direction like fluffy snow.

Melanie's eyes swung to the hallway, her demeanor suddenly serious. "Get up. Get up quick!" she hissed.

The urgency in her voice propelled me to action. With

the skill of an Olympic gymnast, I rolled to my knees and onto my feet, throwing my arms in the air as if I'd just finished a routine.

Drew appeared in the entrance to my cubicle and surveyed the disaster; hundreds of sheets of paper covered the floor, my desk, the chairs, the shelves. And interspersed among the mess were the wadded up paper balls.

At least all the airplanes were hidden.

I dropped my arms to my sides.

"Everything okay in here?" Drew said with a friendly smile.

My stomach flopped at the sight of him in jeans and a white dress shirt like he'd been wearing the night before at dinner. I gave myself a mental slap. I couldn't be attracted to him. Not if he turned me in. Not until I knew for sure that he wasn't behind the reprimand from human resources. I bent to one side and then the other. "Just stretching, getting the kinks out."

Melanie began to scoop sheets from the floor and straighten them into piles. "Kristin was carrying a stack of papers and slipped." She gestured upward with both hands to demonstrate how the whole thing unfolded.

I knelt down to help. "We're sorting old files for Carly."

Drew gathered some sheets that had flown into the hallway and handed them to me. I added them to my pile, straightening the edges and smoothing a palm across the top.

"Any luck finding that research I asked about?" He leaned casually against the doorframe of my cubicle.

I wracked my brain for a reasonable way to ask if he was the person who reported my website to human resources. "I'm, um, still working on it."

"No problem. I was just meeting with Carly and thought I'd check before heading to the airport."

"I have some calls to make," Melanie said, escaping down the hall. "I'll come back later to finish."

Suddenly, I was determined to get to the truth. My heart started to pound. "I had a meeting with the HR director this morning about the website..." I paused, wanting to choose my next words carefully so they didn't come across like an accusation.

"That was fast. I only just talked to him."

"You talked to him?" The room swam and I put my hand on my desk to steady myself. "Why didn't you say something last night? At least give me a heads up so I could be prepared."

He looked a little sheepish. "Protocol. Procedure. That's an HR role. I'm already making so many changes around here, I want to stick to policy whenever possible. Appears less like micromanaging that way."

I nodded, unable to speak. What kind of man went straight to the nuclear option without first seeing if something else might work better—something simple like telling me to take the site down.

Suddenly I realized what it meant when he stood in the rain and watched me drive away.

Nothing.

It meant nothing.

Disbelief spread through my brain, wrapping itself around my thoughts like tentacles, and crushing my hopes of any future with the catalog. Or with Drew.

"I take it...no objections?" he asked.

"No, of course not." I forced my lips into a smile. The idea of telling him off hovered on the tip of my tongue, tempting me with its promise of immediate gratification. But if there was one thing I knew for sure, telling the company president to *fuck off* was no way to keep my job.

So I did the next best thing.

"I have to admit, I'm struggling to find the research I told you about last night," I said in a cool voice. "Maybe it's already been disproven, and people took the studies down." I shrugged. "Maybe I got it backward, and I'm remembering what I hoped the studies showed—not what they actually showed. Wouldn't be the first time I got something wrong."

My mind spooled back to those continental breakfasts I'd gone to with a goal of meeting one—just one—secure, stable guy. And what had I found? Yet another man who needed saving. Despite the fact that Drew thought he'd gotten out of high finance without losing his soul, he had brought home a cutthroat edge.

My heart started to crumble. No, it wasn't the first time I got something wrong. Especially as it related to guys.

~

That night, we took down the website.

"Think of it this way," Bree said. "You never have to worry again that Drew might think Get Outa Town is fake. It's so real to him, he's threatened by it."

"It's just hard to believe he would do this." Megan was at the computer entering the information necessary to drop the site. She looked at me, fingers still on the keyboard. "If it helps at all, Get Outa Town accomplished exactly what you needed it to. It kept Drew from discovering you lied about being a reviewer."

"Right," I muttered. "Except for the betrayal. I can't shake the sense of betrayal. Sunday night, he acts like I'm an integral part of the team. Monday morning, I'm trying to cheat the company...or something. I just don't understand why he didn't say something himself."

"It's probably the micromanaging thing. People are complaining," Megan said. "He's bending over backward to avoid overstepping on day-to-day stuff. Personnel deals with personnel issues—not the company president who's been brought in to turn the place around. He may decide who gets fired, but he doesn't do the firing. Or, in this case, the reprimanding."

I nodded, disheartened. "It doesn't help that I'd started to think that we were developing a...friendship."

"We all thought it." Allie put a reassuring hand on my arm.

"He said he got disillusioned by all the duplicity on Wall Street."

"Apparently, he's not disillusioned by it when it serves his own purposes," Bree said. "Consider yourself lucky to have learned about him so early on."

I waited until late the next day to send Drew an email, formal and carefully-worded, saying I had done everything I could to find the studies and articles I'd told him about, but hadn't had any luck. I apologized for bringing the ideas forward without the data to back them up and asserted my commitment to helping The Joneses transition to the vision he and the board had laid out. He sent a one-sentence reply two hours later, obviously from his smartphone, thanking me for my efforts and saying he wouldn't be back in the office until late Friday.

And that was that. I did my job. I watered my plants and picked vegetables. I saw my friends. And every once in a while, my thoughts wandered back to that moment when Drew leaned through my open car window in the rain. And then I would kick myself for ever thinking it meant something.

FOURTEEN

The weekend and *Taste of Twin Cities* brought welcome change from my regular day-to-day life. I had promised Nate that Allie and I would swing by his stand to see how things were going; but once we completed that last responsibility, I was done freelancing for him. After tonight, I didn't want anything more to do with either brother.

The girls and I arrived early, the plan being that Bree and Allie would spin off later and meet up with their boyfriends. The sky was clear, the breeze soft, and it seemed like everyone who lived in Minneapolis and St. Paul was at *Taste of Twin Cities*.

Some seventy restaurants offering an incredible variety of foods to buy or sample, had set up shop along the streets in the park. A band played on a large stage, several people danced on the grass down in front.

Children with happy, chocolate-smeared chins held tight to helium-filled balloons. Everyone was talking and smiling and laughing. It was just an awesome escape from real life.

The four of us tasted our way through the event—sliders and ice cream and sushi and gyros and deep dish pizza and cheesecake and cupcakes and—well, you get the idea. Suffice to say, we didn't expect to be hungry again for days.

Allie wiped tomato sauce off her mouth with a napkin. "The guys are going to be here pretty soon. So if we're going to stop at Grandad's, we better do it."

"I'm not sure I have room for a donut," Bree said, holding her stomach.

"You don't have to go, just me and Allie," I said. "And if we spot Drew, we're out of there."

"That's smart. Why give him the chance to jump to another assumption, like you have a booming freelance business?" Megan sighed. "Another violation of your employment contract."

"You got paid in donuts," Bree said.

"Best donuts in the world, but still," Allie said with a sigh.

Bree checked at her phone. "You'd better hurry up. The guys just texted they're at the beer tent."

"Come on, Kristin, let's move it." Allie took off in the direction of Grandad's Donuts.

"Slow down. We don't need to draw attention to

ourselves," I said when I caught up to her. "Do you remember what Drew looks like?"

"Oh yeah. I saw him just fine at the farmers market."

We reached the general vicinity of Grandad's Donuts and took up surveillance from behind a lemonade truck with yellow and green striped awnings. The tart scent of lemon wafted through the air, and we watched the high school kids behind the counter make fresh lemonade one glass at a time, vigorously mixing ice, water, sugar and fresh squeezed lemon juice in a shaker, then pouring it out into a clear plastic glass.

I licked my dry lips, and almost bought a glass but decided if we had to make a run for it, I'd be better off unencumbered. I peered past the stand toward the throng of people at Grandad's Donuts. Two teenagers in white baker aprons were out in front handing out donut samples, while Nate and a woman, also wearing white aprons, filled orders from behind the counter. "I don't see Drew anywhere, do you?"

Allie started toward the stand. "He's probably not even here. Let's make our appearance so we can go to the beer tent."

"Hey!" Nate waved as we got near.

"You look busy," I said happily.

"It's been non-stop." He put a hand on the back of the woman working alongside him. "This is my wife, Libby," he said. "Honey, this is the crackerjack marketing team I've been telling you about—"

"You're Allison and Kristine?" Her face lightened with a wide smile. "I love the donut names—"

"Is it making a difference?" Allie asked.

Nate let out a laugh. "Yeah, we've been nonstop all day. An editor with the paper even stopped by earlier and did an interview."

"He tried every sample," Libby said as she took three tickets from a customer. "Loved every one."

Drew filled an order for two donuts from the next person in line. "He said we'll be featured in a few weeks. This is all because of you two—"

"Not me," Allie said, shaking her head. "Thank Kristine, she's the marketing genius."

"Well, marketing genius, thank you." Nate's eyes swept across the nearby crowd, stopping for a second on a young girl licking her sticky fingers. "See that? We've been so busy, we ran out of napkins. We expected sales to be good, just not this...robust. I want to talk to you about some other stuff, but—" He waved a hand at the lines of customers stretching out from the stand as if to say it would have to be another time.

"We can connect later," I said quickly. I didn't want to talk about doing more work for him. It was really rewarding to know that things were going so well, but this had to be the end of the road. At least now I'd be able to turn him down via email instead of face to face.

"We have to meet some people at the beer tent, anyway," Allie said, handing me an immediate out. She took a couple of steps backward to give the impression that there was some urgency to us leaving.

"We'll get out of here and let you guys keep selling donuts. Nice meeting you, Libby," I called over my shoulder as I followed Allie toward the lemonade truck, eager to disappear into the crowd.

Allie was tapping a text into her phone. "Jax wants to know what kind of beer you want."

"He'll have it waiting?" At that moment, nothing sounded better than an ice-cold beer with my friends. A celebration of sorts, me reclaiming my life.

"Of course."

"I've got to find a guy like him. Tell him anything but a dark beer. They're too heavy for—"

"Kristine!" A hand grabbed my elbow and I jumped, startled.

"Sorry," Nate said. "Hey, I want you to meet someone. Drew, this is the marketing person I was telling you about."

I froze, caught in a snare that was obviously of my own making. My gaze landed on a maintenance man pushing a wheeled dolly loaded with two cardboard boxes: *white paper napkins* was imprinted on one, *white bakery bags* was imprinted on the other.

A baseball cap and dark sunglasses did nothing to hide the fact that this was no ordinary maintenance man. Jack-of-all trades, company president, handy-dandy delivery truck driver, and who knew what the hell else, this was

Drew Lawson about to screw up my life again. I waited for the chaos to begin.

"This is your marketing professional?" Drew took off his sunglasses and lifted the brim of his cap.

I bristled at his words, but my offense was quickly replaced by dread. Drew now knew I wasn't holding just two jobs—I was holding three. Any intelligent person might surmise that a termination was in my near future.

Nate grinned and nodded. "Kristine, meet my business partner. My brother, Drew."

"Kristin's been helping you?" Drew sounded stunned.

"It's *Kristine*," Nate said. "Kristine Carlotta. She's the brains behind our new brand."

Drew frowned at me. "You're working for Nate?"

"Yeah, and she's amazing," Nate said.

"She works at The Joneses. She also runs the review website I told you about. Get Outa Town—"

"Kristine did our review?" Nate's brow furrowed in confusion, and I was pretty sure he was remembering the day Allie and I came into the shop, ate donuts like there was no tomorrow, and told him he should rename everything.

He rubbed a hand over the back of his neck. "You're the reviewer? Kristine, why didn't you say anything?"

"Her name is Kristin." Drew cocked his head. "Unless I've been calling you the wrong name all this time."

My blood was running so cold, my jaw had frozen and my lips wouldn't move. The chickens were about to come home to roost unless I could explain the whole two name thing in a rationale and reasonable way.

The problem was, I couldn't think of one thing to say.

And then Allie, bless her, leapt into the gaping hole. "She goes by both names. One is the Italian version and one is the, uh, Anglicized version. Of the same name. Which is, of course, Kristin. Or Kristine. Whichever you prefer. And Carlotta is the Italianized version of Caruso."

She waved her hands and blabbered every thought that must be popping into her mind. "Or else it's the other way around. But really, she's the same person. Just what you call her can be slightly different, depending, you know, on what, ah, country you're in at the time, or even your preference on a given day, or even her preference. Sometimes, I know, when she's feeling especially romantic, well then she might use Kristin because it's very, um... Italian, I think, or maybe French, but if she wants to be taken seriously, for her mind instead of her body, she will switch to Kristine, which is from the Greek, Kristianopolos, which means trustworthy and pure, but either way, you can see she's the same person."

Kristianopolos? Was that even a name? *Trustworthy and pure?* More like pure embellishment. But Allie said everything with such conviction, I think the two guys believed her. Hell, I almost did, and I knew she was making it all up on the spot. As she stopped to replenish her air supply, my jaw finally thawed. This fiasco was coming to an end right now.

"Actually my name is Kristin. Kristin Carlotta Caruso," I said. All around us was sound—the music from the band, people laughing and talking—but the space between the four of us was hollow with silence. "I told Nate my name was Kristine because…" Oh, I couldn't get into the whole thing about continental breakfast, I just couldn't. "I thought if he knew I worked at The Joneses, it might get awkward…since you two are brothers… I thought it would be simpler to keep the two jobs separate."

"Why would it matter?" Nate asked.

I bit my lip. "At the time, it seemed to make sense."

"So you're working three jobs, not two?" Drew's disbelief was clear in his voice. "How do you have time?"

All my anger and frustration churned to the surface. "Yes. I was working three jobs—two of them very part-time and at night. And if that's a conflict of interest you want to fire me over, fine. Go ahead and do it. Working for Nate came about when I was in here doing the review. I gave him some advice—"

"For which she got paid donuts," Allie chipped in. "Which is little more than peanuts. She helped your brother out of the goodness of her heart and what thanks did she get? You make her take down Get Outa Town. How does not having a review online for Grandad's Donuts help Grandad's Donuts?"

Nate scowled at his brother. "You made her take down the review site?"

"Why would I do that?" Drew cocked his head at me. "You took down the review site?"

I stared at him for a long moment. "What did you think was going to happen when you complained about my blog to the director of human resources?"

Nate waved a hand. "I don't know what's going on here, but I have a booth with no napkins and a ton of donuts to sell. You two figure this out. I'll catch up later." He took the wheeled dolly from Drew and headed toward the stand.

"Kristin, I'm having trouble following," Drew said. "Why would HR make you take down your site?"

Allie snorted. "You're good."

Drew looked from Allie to me. "What the hell is going on?"

"When the director called me in to say I was in violation of my employment contract, I said I would shut down the blog—"

"Wait, wait. HR did what?"

"What did you think would happen when you turned her in?" Allie asked in a snarky voice.

With her help I would be out of a job before another dozen donuts were sold.

Drew wagged a finger at her. "You, in the peanut gallery, give me a minute to figure out what's going on." He leveled his attention on me again. "First of all, I didn't turn you in to HR. Why would I do that? I told HR about Get Outa Town because I wanted you considered for the digital marketing team that's going to develop and run our new, expanded website."

My mouth dropped open.

"Oh my God," Allie whispered.

"And second, what the hell are you violating with your employment contract?"

"You were going to give me a new job?"

"I was trying," he practically growled.

I screwed up my face, then told him about the clause that required management approval to hold another job. "I shut down the site to avoid any suggestion of conflict of interest."

"And did he say anything about a position on the digital marketing team?"

I looked up at him, and all I could see was sincerity in those beautiful brown eyes. Drew hadn't turned me in. Inside, I feel an explosion of hope. "All he said was that I had to fill out paperwork to get approval from the executive board."

Drew's jaw tightened. "No mention of a new job?"

I shook my head.

"He sounds as bad as Carly," Allie chimed in.

I gave her a warning glare. If Drew really wanted me on the digital team, I'd soon be out from under Carly, so why open that can of worms?

"You don't like Carly?" Drew asked.

Allie glared back at me and stuck her hands on her hips, as if to say, *If not now, when*? "I may not work at The

Joneses, but while you're holding all those meetings to find out what every department does, why don't you pay attention to how some people don't play so well with others?"

Drew reached a hand toward me. "Do you have any thoughts on this?"

I groped for the right words, something damning but not bitchy. "Well...sometimes Carly...it seems like she thinks that if someone else gets something good, that means something must have been taken away from her."

Allie's mouth was puckered like she'd bitten into a lemon. I knew she wanted me to cut loose, but I thought a measured response was the better choice since I didn't know how Drew would react to the information or what he would do with it.

"She didn't share, care, and cooperate?" Drew asked.

Despite the seriousness of the moment, I smiled. "Not hardly."

"Let's call it what it is," Allie burst out. "She keeps her employees down. She stole Kristin's idea about changing the catalog into something people won't want to throw away—with articles and all that."

I held up a hand to stop her from saying more. As much as I wanted to see Carly get hers, I couldn't risk this conversation coming back to bite me.

A muscle tensed in Drew's jaw. "That was your idea?"

I studied the ground for a moment. "I told her at least half a year ago."

Drew gave a sharp laugh. "Even though I might have seemed oblivious to interactions in those meetings—especially to people who weren't even there—" He lay a pointed look on Allie and she had the good sense to seem chagrined.

"One of my main purposes was to see how staff worked together," he said. "If I was going to turn the place around, I didn't want any drama, rivalries, power struggles—past, present, or future—happening in the background. I needed employees who played well in the sandbox."

Hahaha, that isn't Carly, I thought to myself.

"That wasn't Carly," Drew said.

Allie's eyes bugged out. I'm sure mine were just as bad.

"The drama she creates is the last thing we needed moving forward. We let her go at the end of the day yesterday." His mouth set in a hard line. "And I can promise you, the director of human resources will be the next to go. I told him about your website because I wanted to promote you—not get you in trouble."

FIFTEEN

CARLY WAS GONE? JOY CASCADED OVER ME LIKE SHEETS OF
water from a thousand dollar showerhead. I pictured how
Melanie and James would react when they learned the
news. First, we'd probably have a group scream. Well, at
least Melanie and I would. James would probably get a bag
of Doritos. Then we would celebrate because a position
had finally opened up in the department. Of course,
Melanie or James would be the obvious choice to succeed
Carly, and their promotion would open a position for new
assistant buyer. *Me.*

For the first time I might actually have options, choices
—digital marketing team or assistant buyer! I touched
Drew's arm and grinned up at him. "You just made this
one of the best weekends of my life.

"She was that bad?"

"Yeah. But also because her leaving means there's

finally..." I faltered, not sure how to say what I was feeling without sounding presumptuous. "There's finally a way for other people to move up, too. Don't get me wrong, joining the digital marketing team sounds amazing, but I really love working on the merchandising and promotion end of things."

Drew's mouth turned down at the corners.

Now what? I was good enough for the digital marketing team but not good enough to be an assistant buyer? Seriously?

Allie slid her phone in front of me so I could see a photo sent by Jax, two clear plastic cups of fresh-poured beer with foamy white heads. "We're getting paged," she chirped.

"Can Kristin catch up with you in a minute?" Drew asked. "I promise I won't keep her long."

"Keep her as long as you like," she said with a happy smirk before taking off.

Drew and I went to sit at a picnic table out of the main walkway; twigs from a nearby tree littered its surface. "Kristin, when you first told me your ideas for the catalog, okay, I'll admit, I wasn't sold. But I liked you. I trusted you. I figured I had nothing to lose by looking at the studies." He picked up one of the sticks and began to break it into smaller pieces. "But when I got your email saying you couldn't find anything, that's when I realized how much I really wanted what you'd said to be true."

I shifted nervously, remembering how I'd dumped all my findings into my computer garbage can.

"So I ran some Internet searches myself." He started to lay the broken twig pieces in a row alongside one another. "Found research that shows people are searching for meaning. Looking for ways to make the world a better place. Discovering that happiness comes from helping others, not hoarding for themselves." He smiled at me. "You were right—the catalog needs a bigger heart."

My mouth dropped open.

"Everything I read confirmed what you told me. I took an earlier flight home so I could meet with the board and all the department heads. Told them you had an idea that might transform The Joneses."

"Me? You mentioned me by name?" I burbled.

He nodded. "I presented the data, then proposed that thirty percent of the next catalog be devoted to things people can buy to make the world a better place. If customer response is promising, I proposed we increased the percentage. Then I opened the floor to discussion."

Tears pricked at the back of my eyes. This man believed in my idea so much that he ran with it? And gave me credit? "What did they say?" I managed to get out without my voice betraying my emotion.

"It was spirited, that's for sure. It's a big change. But after hearing all the details, almost everyone was open to giving it a try." His mouth tightened into a line. "Except a few people. They seemed to be searching for reasons to oppose. Carly was one of them, playing devil's advocate as if her life depended on it. As I listened to her comments, watched her work the table to form alliances with the sole purpose of undermining me... Hell, it was like watching a reality TV show."

"That is so Carly." I didn't try to hide my sarcasm. "You probably guaranteed her resistance just by mentioning my name."

"Well, she's gone now. And you may have saved the company." He grinned. "Of course we'll be monitoring sales, but I'm betting—"

"Hey Drew, heads up!" Nate yelled from the stand. "Come on, man, coffee break's over!"

We turned simultaneously; the lines at the donut stand had gotten so long some people were walking away.

"Damn, I'd better get back to work."

I watched him jog to the donut stand, my heart warmed by the unbelievable thought that the president of The Joneses had listened to, and advocated for, an idea from a lowly merchandising assistant, one of the unrecognizables. This man, who by definition should be just one more self-impressed head of a company, had no qualms about driving a donut delivery truck or standing behind a counter selling donuts or...valuing the thoughts of employees.

He jumped behind the counter and got to work, but the lines were growing faster than the three of them could fill orders. That wasn't good; every person who walked away without a Grandad's Donut was one less new customer to spread the word.

I glanced to either side as if extra staff would suddenly materialize out of the crowds. It wasn't complicated work —just hand people a donut and collect the tickets. Didn't even have to do math or make change. All they needed were more hands.

And I had two of them.

I stood. And promptly sat down again.

Not a month ago, I'd been determined to change my life. Had vowed—*vowed*—to quit inserting myself into other people's problems, to quit trying to save the world.

Just because they needed help at the donut stand didn't mean I should offer to help. They'd probably gape at me like I was crazy and stammer out something dismissive like, "Thanks, but we'll be fine." Which was a nice way of saying, *When we want help, we'll ask for it.*

Except, Drew just said I may have saved the company. Save the world girl might have actually helped save one small world. I reveled in that reality for a moment.

So...maybe it was okay for me to be...me. Obviously not in every situation, of course—I really had to quit dating complete losers who were looking for sugar mommas. But there was nothing wrong with trying to make things better, with standing up for the downtrodden and the helpless. With selling a few donuts.

That's when it hit me. There was nothing wrong with

the way that I was; what was wrong was hating myself for it.

I brushed the pile of twigs off the picnic table and walked over to the donut stand. "Tell me what I can do to help."

Libby smiled at me like I had wings and a halo. Nate pointed at a brown cardboard box under the back counter. "Put on one of those aprons and a pair of latex gloves."

With four of us behind the counter, we quickly took care of the mad rush of customers that had descended all at once. After that, we settled into a more manageable rhythm.

"Drew said you two straightened everything out." Nate handed a plate with three donuts to a young woman and received a handful of tickets in return.

"We did. Lots of good changes coming."

"You want to tell her the rest?" Nate asked his brother.

"Eventually."

Now what? "You can't say something like that and then just let it go," I said in exaggerated indignation.

Drew took an order, then grabbed some donuts and put them in a bag. He waited until there was a letup in customers, then said, "Kristin, when you said that thing about how so many people feel unfulfilled because their lives don't seem to have meaning...you might as well have been talking about me."

"Wall Street," I said, remembering what he'd told me about his years there. "*We're here to make money—*"

"*Not save the world*," he finished. "I took over at The Joneses not because my dad wanted to retire, but because I wanted to quit what I was doing. The Joneses was an escape."

I took two half-pints of milk from the cooler for a customer. "What's wrong with escape?"

"Nothing. As long as you escape into something that matters to you."

Nate waved a hand as if to speed his brother along. "The bottom line is, what Drew really wants to do is—"

"Sell donuts every day," Libby said with flourish.

I laughed, appreciating her sense of humor. "Just promise me one thing, Drew, that you won't let your successor cancel the donut cart."

"I'm not leaving immediately," he said.

"I'm kidding," I said in alarm. "Aren't you?"

Drew stepped to the counter to wait on some customers, and didn't reply until there was a lull. "I'm staying at The Joneses for a year, hopefully long enough get it on a good path to recovery. But Nate and I are partners—"

"You're really going to sell donuts?" I didn't even try to hide my disappointment as I looked from Drew to Nate.

Libby rolled her eyes. "Quit playing twenty questions, guys, and just lay it out."

Drew went to the back of the stand, away from the counter, and motioned for me and Nate to follow. "It's bigger than that," he said in quiet voice. "We're going to expand nationally."

"A gradual roll-out beginning in the Midwest," Nate added.

"I've met with a couple of investors already," Drew said. "But we have a lot to get done first. A business plan to write, proposals to develop, locations to scout—"

"Staff to be added. We need people who think big, who aren't afraid to speak up—"

"What he means is, we need you, Kristin." Drew smiled at me.

I blinked. Several times. I wiped my hands on my apron to have something to do as I tried to sort out what he meant. Libby was watching me, a big grin on her face. What? Were they offering me a job? I opened my mouth to ask for clarification, but before I could get a word out, Nate said, "Director of marketing."

"Director of marketing?" I repeated on exhale.

"You've been wanting a promotion, haven't you?" Drew asked.

Yeah, oh yeah baby, but shit, director of marketing? I nodded, speechless.

"We like the way you think. Smart. Creative. Focused. Your ideas for Grandad's Donuts have been spot on." Nate clapped a congratulatory hand on my shoulder.

"Not to mention, for The Joneses," Drew added.

I couldn't think straight. They wanted me to be part of their expansion? Wanted to move me from merchandising assistant to director of marketing? How could they have that kind of faith in me? Don't get me wrong, I was totally capable, but these guys barely knew me. Okay, yeah, I came up with some great ideas for rebranding the donuts, okay and even for rebranding The Joneses, but, well—

"The clincher for us was this. Most people who think about starting a business don't even get past the idea stage," Drew was saying. "You had the drive, initiative, and determination to come up with an idea, launch a business you believed in, and make it a success."

Whaaat?

"Get Outa Town cemented it for us. We want to harness your resourcefulness and put it to work for Grandad's Donuts."

Oh fuck.

Drew patted me on the shoulder. "You'll be involved in every aspect of expansion planning over the next year, an integral player in the roll-out."

My stomach twisted. My *resourcefulness* had nothing to do with starting a business I believed in and everything to do with hiding the truth from Drew.

"Reinforcements needed," Libby called.

I wiped my hands on my apron and followed the guys back to the counter, mentally scrolling through one thought after another. I really didn't want to keep lying about Get Outa Town. But the unvarnished truth was so ugly...

"So, Kristin, are you in?" Nate asked once we'd caught

up the customers again. "Or do you need some time to think it over?"

I didn't need any time. I wanted this job more than anything in the world, but I wouldn't be able to live with myself if I took it under false pretenses. I stepped back from the counter. My eyes flicked over the *Taste of Twin Cities* crowd as I gathered my courage. "It sounds wonderful. And I would love to explore it further, but..." A knot wadded itself in my throat and I blinked back the moisture that had sprung to my eyes. "Everything isn't exactly as it seems," I said in a low voice. "And you guys should know the truth before you make any job offers."

"The truth will set you free," Drew quipped.

A wry half-laugh, half-sob slipped out of me. Yeah, free and jobless. Not only would I lose this opportunity, but I'd probably lose my job at The Joneses, too—or at least any chance of moving up. "Remember that morning we met at continental breakfast?"

Drew nodded.

I wrapped my arms around my waist. "Well, I wasn't there to review the restaurant. I was there to...meet single men."

"You mean, you're an—an—escort?"

"No! Oh God, no. No, no, no. You're misunderstanding." I dove into a description of The Continental Breakfast Club, explaining how I'd tried to maximize my success by going to four different hotels in four days, and how, once Drew assumed I was a reviewer, I'd agreed with him because I thought he was a security guard, and that way I wouldn't have to admit what I was really doing there.

"So, if you're not a reviewer, why do you have a review site?" Nate asked.

Here it came, the beginning of the end. "Right. So, when I discovered the man I'd met at breakfast was the new president of The Joneses, and that I'd not only lied to him but also ditched him that morning, and he was going to do a company-wide reorganization and people were going to lose their jobs, well, it just seemed to make sense..."

I prayed a lightning bolt would strike me dead before I had to admit to any more of my choices. I waited, waited, waited for that golden bolt of electricity to arrive, but of course it didn't. When did luck ever go my way?

"What made sense?" Nate asked.

"You have to understand that my MasterCard bill is pretty high—and I take full responsibility for that," I said, my voice beginning to tremble. "But if I lost my job, I would probably lose my apartment and have to move in with my parents because I don't make enough money to save much—my savings account is pitiful actually—and even though my parents are nice people—"

"They're great," Drew interjected.

"Right, they're great. But who wants to return to the same bedroom they grew up in?"

"You've lost me." Drew shook his head.

"In your speech the very first day, you said you

valued integrity, you wanted less duplicity and more trust." My voice rose with emotion. Tears overflowed my lower lashes and I dashed a hand across my eyes. "I mean, you put the definition of integrity up on the giant screen. It's branded into my memory. *Integrity: the quality of being honest and fair. Sincerity. Truthfulness. Trustworthiness.*"

"Still lost," Nate said.

Fine. Just fine. "There was no website until two weeks ago. Get Outa Town didn't even exist." Blood was rushing in my ears. "I made the site so Drew wouldn't discover I'd lied to him at breakfast that morning. So I wouldn't have to admit that what I was really doing...was stealing breakfast to try to meet single men."

Dead silence met my pronouncement. Finally Nate said, "Let me make sure I have this right. You created a fake website to convince Drew of your integrity so you wouldn't get fired because of lack of integrity."

That sounded really bad.

I gave a nod.

"And the reviews?" Drew asked. "Those are fake, too?"

"No, no! Those are real," I said, my voice shaking again as I looked between the two guys. They had to believe me, especially Nate. "Remember that Sunday morning Allie and I came into the shop? We were doing research for the review. The site's a fake, but the reviews are all real. I didn't want to put anything up that might hurt someone else's business."

Nate nodded slowly. "I guess this brings us to a really important question," he said in a low, serious voice.

I knew exactly what that question was: Based on all my actions, how could I ever be trusted?

I pressed my lips together to keep them from quivering. I wanted to assure them that, yes, I could be trusted, that I did have integrity. I wanted to say I would work harder for them than they could imagine. I wanted to grovel and beg and promise. But I did none of that. Whatever happened, I deserved it. This nightmare was the result of choices I'd made. A tear rolled over my cheekbone and I just let it be.

Nate nodded again. "And that question is, did you meet anyone at continental breakfast worth seeing again?"

What? *What?*

My mind stammered as it searched for a reply. I couldn't even look at Drew right then, let alone admit the truth.

Could I?

It suddenly dawned on me that it didn't matter if they knew the truth. Every piece of my deception was crumbling around me; why lie anymore?

"One guy. I met one," I said quietly as I raised my eyes to Drew. "And all I want is for him to forgive me."

No one spoke for a long time. Nate cleared his throat. "I don't know, Drew, but anyone who does that well starting a business for all the wrong reasons, well imagine the results they'd get if they applied their talents for all the right reasons."

Drew was staring at me with the same expression he'd had that night in the rain. "I don't give a shit about why you made the website." His voice was low and rough. "I get it. I understand how one step leads to another, until you're so far along a path you never planned to take in the first place you can't find your way back."

"I'm sorry," I whispered. "For all of it."

"The morning we met when I asked you to come over to Grandad's Donuts? It wasn't because I wanted a review for Nate." He gave an apologetic shrug. "It was because I wanted to talk to you some more, and it seemed less creepy than asking for your number."

Nate filled a bag with donuts for a customer. "Someday, ask me to tell you what he said when he discovered that the woman he'd met at continental breakfast—the one whose name he never got—worked at The Joneses."

"Shut up, Nate." Drew skewered his brother with a warning look. "Okay, here it is. I like the way your brain works. I like the directions it takes you. I like that you aren't afraid to save the world."

The lump in my throat expanded.

He turned both hands palm up. "And now that I've had the chance to talk to you a little more, I can tell you one thing, it's still not enough—whichever way you're going, I want to come along."

I started to laugh and cry at the same time, and Drew pulled me into his arms and kissed me, soft and tender and wanting and full of promise.

As we pulled apart, the people in line waiting for donuts started to clap.

"I think this calls for a celebration," Nate said to the customers. "Donuts for everyone." He picked up a donut and handed it to Drew. "Here's an Apple Doodle Dandy. And Kristin—what'll you have?"

"My all-time favorite," I said. "Honey glazed."

Nate shook a finger at me. "You should know better than that. It's not honey glazed—it's Sweet Lovin'. How can our Director of Marketing have already forgotten Sweet Lovin'?" he asked in exaggerated dismay.

"You just take care of getting her the donut, Nate," Drew said, as he pulled me close again and his mouth descended toward mine. "I'll make sure she gets all the sweet lovin' she's ever going to want."

If you enjoyed this book ... I would be eternally grateful if you would post a review on the site where you bought it.

Please enjoy the following excerpt from *Love on the Lane*, book one in *The Bachelor Next Door* series.

~

Excerpt from
LOVE ON THE LANE
The Bachelor Next Door, book one

Prologue

Their grandmother had been the last to speak at their grandfather's funeral.

She stepped to the podium and in a quiet voice retold the love story they all knew by heart—and none ever tired of hearing. How she and Grandpa had grown up down the block from one another, how he'd been five years older (practically another generation!), how they'd only known each other in passing, and how a chance encounter made them realize that the person they'd each been looking for had been in front of them all along.

Then she'd turned her gaze to the six young women, all cousins, seated together in a row near the front. "My sweet granddaughters," she said, smiling through her tears, "I have just one bit of wisdom to offer. No matter where you end up, from Maine to California or somewhere in between, make sure you don't search so far and wide you miss out on the bachelor next door."

Chapter One

On a bright Saturday morning in August, Elizabeth Gordon opened her mail, spilled her coffee and came face-to-face with her life. It wasn't pretty.

The dark liquid streamed across the letter she had laid open on the kitchen table and poured over the edge like a waterfall to the scuffed hardwood floor below. She jumped to her feet and snatched a handful of napkins from the holder, blotting at the spill as though she could lift the words from that single sheet and make them disappear. As if it would make her forget what she had just read ...

Dear Izzy,

If you've gotten this letter, it means you're coming up to your ten-year high school reunion. Can you believe it, Iz? You've been out of high school ten years already. So, here's what you're doing for a living right now: you're a movie director. Or, okay, maybe an assistant director. That'd be all right too. Or even an assistant-to-an-assistant.

As long as you're doing what you want to do—and not what Mom and Dad want. Tell me you didn't marry some guy they thought was perfect and become a trophy wife. On a shelf. With 2.5 perfect kids.

Because, Izzy, if you did, I don't know what I'll do. I'm eighteen. I'm about to graduate from high school and go to college. I don't want a husband. I want to do something fun, exciting, rewarding. I want to work in film. You want to work in film. So, Izzy, that's your future. The movies!

I can't wait to get there. I can't wait to read this in ten years and know that I'm doing something I love—just like they said I couldn't.

Love and kisses, xxxooo from yourself,
Izzy

It had been an English class assignment her senior year—write a letter to yourself describing what your life would be like in ten years. The teacher had collected the letters and said they would be mailed out with the reunion invitation.

She'd forgotten all about it. Slowly she lowered herself into her chair. *What had happened to her dreams?* Somehow she'd fallen into a lifestyle—pattern—*rut*. How had she let her life come to this, this moment where her loss of direction seemed exquisitely obvious? Suddenly she had the sensation that she was floating, looking down at herself like they say you do when you die.

"Izzy?"

She snapped back into her body and focused on the willowy blonde in the doorway, her roommate Shelly Kent. Though her name was actually Michelle, she'd been called Shelly ever since her little brother had been unable to pronounce her name as a toddler. With her fine-boned features, Shelly could have been a model, but she rarely wore makeup outside of work and paid just enough attention to fashion to make sure she wasn't out of style.

"The mail came already?" Barefoot and wrapped in a fluffy pink robe, Shelly padded toward her and reached for the small pile of bills and junk mail.

"Yeah." Years were passing her by and she hadn't even noticed. *Dreams were passing her by.* She'd meant to get into film and instead ... She cringed.

"What's the matter with you?" Shelly glanced up from the mail. "Did you get on the scale this morning? Because I thought we decided we'd only weigh in every—"

"I'm the traffic manager at a little cable TV station," Izzy said with disdain. *"Traffic manager."*

"So?"

"So? I manage the video inventory. I maintain the advertising logs. I schedule on-air promotion. I don't do anything remotely related to making movies."

"And I'm the weather girl. A weather girl—not a movie star."

"Yeah, but traffic manager was never on my list of dreams. Weather girl was on yours."

"Only if I didn't make it as a movie star. And you may have noticed, Hollywood hasn't come calling yet, although when they do, I'll be ready. Until then, it's cumulus clouds for me." Shelly poured herself a cup of coffee, refilled Izzy's mug, and slid into the seat opposite. "I'm sure traffic manager is on somebody's list of dreams—just add it to yours. So, what's this really about?"

Izzy picked up the damp letter and slapped it on the table in front of Shelly. "Read this. How would you feel if you got *this* in the mail?"

As Shelly read the letter, she pressed her lips into a tight line. "Like a loser. Especially if I got to my reunion and discovered everyone else had succeeded beyond their wildest dreams."

"Thanks."

"I'm just kidding." Shelly pushed her chin-length hair behind one ear and took a sip of her coffee. "I'm sure it won't be like that. When you're eighteen you don't know anything about life or what it takes to succeed. You didn't have a clue how hard it would be to break into directing—"

"I hardly tried. My parents knew the manager at the cable station, so I landed there—and stayed. Dreams be damned, it was just easier. You were right the first time. *Loser.* At least I have a boyfriend."

Shelly made a gagging sound. Tilting her head, she considered Izzy thoughtfully for a long moment. Then she shoved back her chair, rolled up her robe sleeves, and began to pick through the garbage in the wastebasket beneath the sink.

"There's food in the pantry. Just because we're dieting doesn't mean you have to resort to scraps."

"Haha. I finally sorted through that mountain of old junk mail and magazines on my nightstand yesterday," Shelly said, still digging. "And wouldn't you know it, today I need something I threw away. You always wonder why I keep that stuff for so long, well, this is why. Because—here it is!" She pulled a brochure from the bag and wiped a swath of coffee grounds off the front.

"Here what is?"

"Your salvation. The Americana Documentary Film Contest for amateur and student filmmakers."

Mug halfway to her mouth, Izzy froze. "What?"

"Now, if we have any luck at all ..." Shelly opened the brochure and scanned the copy. "Thank God. The Outline Submission Round doesn't close for four days."

Izzy almost choked on her coffee. "Are you out of your mind?"

"Do you want to go to your class reunion as the person who didn't even try to follow her dreams? They'll probably present everyone's letters and goals in some big PowerPoint presentation—or posters hanging on the walls." Shelly waved a hand through the air. "I can almost see it. Column one—what each person wanted to do. Column two—a gold star for those who succeeded and a sad face for you, because the one thing you accomplished was the only thing you told yourself *not* to do—settle down with some guy your parents thought was perfect."

Izzy stared, flabbergasted, as her friend kept talking without waiting for an answer.

"Let's try this, Izzy. All we need to do is submit a one-to-two-page summary proposal describing the documentary film we plan to make if we get chosen to progress to the Video Submission Round."

"We?"

Shelly grinned. "*We,* baby. You want to be a director. I want to be a star. We might as well chase our dreams together."

Izzy snorted out a laugh. "Go back to bed and get some more sleep. You're delirious."

"Delirious? Replace the *r* with a *c* and I'm *delicious.*"

"Ohmigod."

"Face it, Iz, it's an absolutely delicious idea. And since we're practically starving ourselves to lose ten pounds, *delicious* is a word I'd like to have in my vocabulary right now even if it only relates to making a movie."

This was absurd. Totally and absolutely absurd. And totally and absolutely tempting. "What happens if we progress to the Video Submission Round?"

"I thought you'd never ask." Shelly turned her attention back to the brochure. "Two weeks after the Outline Submission Round closes, ten entrants will be selected as finalists by a panel of judges," she read aloud.

"Finalists will then have two months to create a six-minute short documentary expressing the topic presented in their outline."

The idea began to cozy its way deeper into Izzy's mind. "And the winners are announced ... when?"

Shelly dropped into her chair and tossed the brochure on the table. "Ten days after that. This whole contest will be wrapped up in three months—in plenty of time for your class reunion. Feels like it was meant to be, doesn't it?"

"I'm merely asking a few questions. I'm not actually considering it. I mean, what would Andrew think?"

"Andrew would think you're being silly and impulsive, that you don't have a prayer of winning so why enter, that if you become a finalist you won't have as much free time to be the perfect girlfriend to him." Shelly straightened in her chair and raised her mug. "Who cares what Andrew thinks?"

"Well, I—"

"No! No, you don't! Come on, Izzy, it's the chance of a lifetime. You get to follow your dreams and I get to be in front of a camera discussing something other than weather patterns."

Izzy pursed her lips and silently debated whether her roommate was brilliant or deranged. There was such a fine line between the two.

"It could be a real bonus for your career. I mean, think if we won. Doors would open—"

"*Could* open." Izzy stood and refilled her mug. Shelly could be on to something. Or not. She did have a penchant for jumping to wild conclusions.

"*Probably* open. For both of us. No more traffic managing for you. No more weather girl for me." She arched a hand through the air. "From now on it'll be top billing for both of us! Come on, Izzy, help me out here."

"Shelly, what if—"

"We submit a proposal. What could possibly go wrong?"

Actually, she couldn't think of a thing, short of Andrew getting exasperated with her. But if they finaled, Andrew's exasperation would be the least of her concerns. The corners of her lips curved upward as she considered what it would feel like to attend her reunion with her head held high, as a finalist—maybe even the winner—of a documentary film contest.

"Come on, what have we got to lose?" Shelly urged.

Nothing. Izzy exhaled. "Okay, we'll write an outline."

"We will?" Shelly jumped to her feet and danced over to wrap her arms around Izzy. "You're the best!"

"Oh, stop. Just two pages, right? On any American topic?"

"That's what it says. Got any thoughts?"

"I don't know ... football? That's pretty American."

Shelly stuck two pieces of wheat bread in the toaster. "Football skews male. What if some of the judges are female? How about something with cooking ... apple pie?"

"Skews female. And boring."

For the next several minutes they bandied about ideas, discarding each in turn for one reason or another.

"What about that property your parents own? That old resort up in Wisconsin." Shelly sprinkled cinnamon and sugar on the toast, and handed a piece to Izzy. "Isn't that place steeped in Americana?"

Izzy shrugged. "They don't own the resort—only the land. And they're selling that, anyway. My great-great-grandfather gave some guy a hundred-year lease and finally it's coming due."

"Hmm. That could be an interesting angle."

"Yeah, well, the broker told my parents it's getting run-down. Who wants to see a documentary about a seedy resort?"

"No one." Shelly's face fell.

Izzy bit into her toast and contemplated their options. A memory of her grandfather telling stories of the old days popped into her mind. "Unless ... what if we don't do a documentary about the resort? What if it's about the gangsters?"

"What gangsters?"

"My grandpa used to tell me stories that his father told him. About growing up there during the twenties. How gangsters from Chicago used to come to northern Wisconsin for vacations and—"

"You mean like Al Capone?"

"Yeah. And John Dillinger and Baby Face Nelson and—"

"Are you kidding me?" Shelly set her coffee cup on the table and leaned forward onto her elbows. "Did they ever stay at your resort?"

"It's not our resort—"

"Yeah, yeah, only the land. Did they ever stay there?"

"That's what he said. Course, he always loved to tell a good yarn."

"Good yarn? *Gangster Getaways in the Wisconsin Northwoods.* Izzy, it's perfect!" Shelly reached excitedly for the contest brochure and knocked over her mug, spilling coffee on the ten-year-old letter once again. As the dark liquid poured over the table edge to pool on the floor beneath, Shelly grabbed a handful of napkins and began to sop up the mess. "Good things are coming our way, Izzy, I can feel it. Clear skies ahead!"

Love on the Lane excerpt
Copyright © 2017 by Pamela Ford

To receive news about upcoming books, giveaways, and special offers join Pamela Ford's mailing list at pamelaford.net.

ABOUT THE AUTHOR

PAMELA FORD is the award-winning author of contemporary and historical romance. She grew up watching old movies, blissfully sighing over the romance; and reading sci-fi and adventure novels, vicariously living the action. The combination probably explains why the books she writes are romantic, happily-ever-afters with plenty of plot—and often, lots of laughter.

After graduating from college with a degree in Advertising, Pam spent many years as a copywriter and freelance writer before inserting a plot twist in her career path and writing her first book.

Pam has won numerous awards including the Booksellers Best, the Laurel Wreath, and a gold medal IPPY in the Independent Book Publisher Awards. She is a National Readers' Choice Awards finalist, a Maggie Awards finalist, a Kindle Book Awards finalist, and a two-time Golden Heart Finalist.

Sign up for Pam's mailing list at: www.pamelaford.net
Contact: pamelafordbooks@gmail.com
Facebook.com/pamelafordbooks
Instagram.com/pamelafordbooks